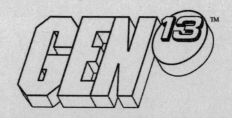

VERSION 2.0

D1570038

VERSION 2.0

SHOLLY FISCH

ILLUSTRATIONS BY MATT HALEY

WILDSTORM PRODUCTIONS

BP BOOKS

ACE BOOKS

GEN[13]: VERSION 2.0

An Ace Book
A BP Books, Inc. Book

PRINTING HISTORY
Ace mass-market edition / June 2002

Visit our website at
www.penguinputnam.com
Check out the ACE Science Fiction & Fantasy newsletter!

Visit the BP Books website at
www.ibooksinc.com

ISBN: 0-441-00946-8

PRINTED IN THE UNITED STATES OF AMERICA

10 9 8 7 6 5 4 3 2 1

This one's for Suze,
the love of my life,
who's been waiting far too long
to have a book dedicated to her.

CHAPTER 1

Two months ago . . .
  Martin Cheswick hated children.

In fact, Martin Cheswick had *always* hated children, even back in the days when he was a child himself. In the slum neighborhood where he grew up, the young Cheswick had been a tubby, unpopular kid—not smart enough to be the teacher's pet, not coordinated enough to be an athlete, and not funny enough to be the class clown. His size and slowness made him an easy target for the petty cruelties of the older, stronger bullies who took delight in tormenting him. Even at the time, Cheswick knew full well that it wasn't that they were after his lunch money or anything like that. It couldn't have been; he never had any to steal. He didn't really understand why they did it. It seemed as though they did it simply for the sake of doing it.

It wasn't until many years later that, in retrospect, Cheswick realized that the main reason for all of his beatings and victimization probably had nothing to do with him personally. Those kids had spent their young lives in the same filthy slum he had. In all likelihood, they made his life a living hell just to help them feel better about their own.

Not that it changed his feelings, of course. With each new humiliation, Cheswick's loathing for the children around him had grown, day by day. But the clincher came in one particular incident that, even forty-five years later, still caused him to fight down a shudder when he thought of it.

Cheswick had taken to experimenting with different ways to leave school at the end of the day, and alternate routes to walk home. He hoped that the roundabout paths would keep him from running into his tormentors. If he could stay out of their sight long enough, then maybe, over time, they'd forget all about him. Or, at least, maybe they'd find a new victim to take his place.

Lately, Cheswick had been ducking down the school's back stairs to slip out a basement exit. He'd circle around the blank wall at the side of the school and head down the alley behind the diner, the tattoo parlor, and the bail bondsman. Once he made it to that point, there was no way to avoid having to come out into the open, but it was only a short sprint across the street before he could squeeze past the fence by the grocery store to reach the back yard of his apartment building and the safety of home.

The route had been working pretty well for the better part of a week—well enough to make him a little too careless—when it happened. Cheswick was halfway down the alley, right between the diner and the tattoo parlor, when he found himself surrounded by the very gang of kids that he'd tried so hard to avoid. (Even as an adult, their smug, mocking voices still echoed in Cheswick's memory.) Despite their cruel smiles, they weren't happy about the tubby kid who thought he could outsmart them. They decided to teach him a lesson.

He was garbage, they said. And there was just one place that garbage belonged. He struggled pointlessly as the bigger kids grabbed him, lifted him up, and physically threw him into the half-full dumpster behind the diner. Before he could react, they slammed the lid and somehow jammed it closed. Cheswick shouted and pounded on the metal as their jeering laughter faded into the distance.

For over an hour, Cheswick was trapped in the dark, thrashing around amid the grease and slime from dozens of cheap meals. The stench of rotting food filled his nostrils, making it difficult to breathe. There was little danger of suffocation; the seal on the rusting dumpster was far from airtight. But that didn't make it any more pleasant.

Still, the smell wasn't the worst part. Thanks to the greasy bits of leftover food, the pitch-black dumpster was infested with countless numbers of cockroaches. The roaches had no particular interest in the human who'd invaded their feeding ground, but at the same time, they had no hesitation about crawling across his body on their way to their afternoon meal. There were too many to kill them all, and it was too dark to be able to stay away from them. His skin clammy with sweat, Cheswick quickly realized that he'd better keep his eyes and mouth tightly closed if he didn't want any of the vermin crawling in accidentally. Tears streamed silently down his cheeks as the terrified youth wore his hands bloody, banging loudly on the lid in an attempt to force it open or at least attract attention. It took forever until the owner of the tattoo parlor finally heard the noise and released the filthy, trembling boy back out into the daylight.

That was why he hated children.

The years had brought many changes to Martin Cheswick. True, he still wasn't particularly athletic or funny, and his doctor hounded him regularly about finally getting serious about a diet. However, as he grew to adulthood, Cheswick had discovered that his shortcomings held little weight in the light of his many successes. He'd grown up to become a powerful, influential man. A man whose decisions affected millions. A man to whom people paid attention. Yet, even so, none of it erased the traumas of the past, and none of it changed the fact that he still hated children.

So why was he visiting an after-school program?

The answer was actually quite simple. Whatever his personal feelings might be, Senator Martin Cheswick was a consummate politician. And this was an election year.

All of which meant that when the invitation came to visit an after-school program designed to keep preteen

children off drugs and off the streets of New York City—
and one supported by private donors instead of the government's bank book, no less—there were no second
thoughts to delay Cheswick's reply. The Senator promised
to be there with bells on.

Not to mention a mass of photographers in tow.

At first, when they pulled up in front of the building,
Cheswick wondered whether it was his driver or his sec-
retary who had made the mistake. He'd never heard of an
after-school program in a Wall Street office building before. To Cheswick, the towering structure of glass and
steel seemed much more suited to mergers and acquisi-
tions than to "rap sessions" and inane babbling about this
week's pop stars. However, his aide did a quick check of
the building directory, and assured him, a moment later,
that they were indeed in the right place. He and Cheswick
rode the elevator up to the seventeenth floor.

Even as they stepped off the elevator and Cheswick
pasted a well-practiced smile across his face, they were
greeted by welcoming committee comprised of three of
the little brats and their teacher. Not surprisingly, the tac-
iturn youngsters let their teacher do all the talking. She
was a slender woman whose glasses and tightly pulled-
back hair accentuated the severity of her features. Her
sensible business suit told Cheswick that she truly was a
teacher by training, and not just another earthy-crunchy
social worker out to save these children from the big, bad
world. He grasped her hand in both of his own and shook
it warmly.

The program itself was housed in a converted office
suite down the hall from the elevator. As though trying
to confirm Cheswick's earlier thought, the teacher acknowledged that it was an unusual location for this sort
of program. But the owner of the building was one of
their benefactors, and one doesn't argue with an offer of
rent-free space in Manhattan.

As they entered the office space that housed the program, an assortment of bored news photographers re-

sponded by lazily raising their cameras into position and setting off the requisite barrage of flash bulbs. Cheswick looked around the main room, nodding as though he genuinely cared about what went on here and approved of the effort. The conversion of the space seemed to have consisted primarily of hanging anti-drug posters on the walls, furnishing the place with game tables and pinball machines, and placing chairs and couches at angles that had been carefully calculated to encourage conversation. About a half-dozen preteen youths were already sitting quietly on mats on the floor, and the three from the hallway silently joined them.

Moving with a smooth confidence, the teacher stepped up in front of the group and began to talk. Well, that cleared up the order of the agenda, at any rate. Realizing that his own turn to speak would come later, Cheswick's first inclination was to remain standing at the side of the room. But if there was one thing that Cheswick's media consultant had drummed successfully into his head, it was to always go for the photo-op. So instead of standing where he was, Cheswick eased himself down to the floor with an awkward grunt to sit among the children. He felt proud of the air of caring and "just plain folks" that he was sure the action conveyed.

By this point, the teacher had already begun to warm to her speech. She droned on and on about the program and the good work it did. She praised the generous backers who made their work possible and made such a difference in the lives of these children.

In short, it was the usual.

Since the odds of finding anything interesting in the speech were roughly equivalent to the chances of finding solid gold nuggets in his shorts, Cheswick decided to pass the time by picturing the teacher naked, instead. Just like in an old, black-and-white movie, he imagined himself tossing away her tortoise shell glasses and letting her dark hair down to fall freely in a cascade over her shoulders.

The suit was next, peeling slowly off her body to reveal the smooth skin beneath.

Actually, Cheswick decided, once you got the teacher out of her all-business attire, she was really quite attractive. In fact, she reminded him of someone. He couldn't quite place who it was, though. Was it someone he knew? He met so many people these days that he couldn't be sure. Or perhaps it was the reference to old movies, bringing up half-remembered images of some actress or something from long ago.

Before he could pin it down, Cheswick snapped out of his daydream at the sound of his name. The teacher was wrapping up her own speech now, and segueing into his introduction. Cheswick struggled a bit to get to his feet, but managed to be standing next to the teacher by the time she extended a hand to wave him on.

Once again, Cheswick shook her hand warmly and took his position before the group of youngsters. He looked out over his audience with a smile that masked the discomfort he felt. It wasn't just the idea of talking to a group of kids; he certainly didn't enjoy that sort of thing, but he had done more than enough of it in the past to be able to deal with it now. No, it was something more specific, something about *these* kids in particular. Usually, he'd found young audiences to react to the presence of a famous politician and camera crew in one of two ways: Either they would get so excited that they couldn't sit still and would spend half the time mugging into the cameras (cutting into his own exposure, he noted with more than a touch of resentment), or they would succumb to stage fright and be silent as stone until the visitors were gone and they resumed their normal routine.

At first, Cheswick had assumed that these children fell into the latter category, and that their silence was simply due to their own nervousness. But now that he was looking at—and more important, genuinely *seeing*—their faces, he realized that there was more to it than that. Their eyes rested obediently upon him, but he didn't detect any signs of anxiety within them. Instead, their expressionless faces seemed to reflect total apathy. As far as Cheswick could tell, the children seemed to regard him with all the interest that they'd give to a wad of used chewing gum on the sidewalk.

Cheswick couldn't tell what was wrong. Did they sense his opinion of them, somehow? Had he said or done something to let his true feelings slip?

Whatever it was, he couldn't afford to drop the ball in front of the cameras. With only a moment's hesitation, he launched into his prepared remarks.

"Ladies and gentlemen, boys and girls, thank you for inviting me to speak here today. It's a pleasure, every once in a while, to have the chance to speak to people with IQs higher than the ones I usually find in Washington."

Cheswick chuckled at his little joke. But he was the only one.

"Seriously, though," he continued, "I am thrilled to have the opportunity to honor the fine work that this center does in offering children alternatives, broadening their horizons, and steering them toward the straight and narrow. As I have often said, children are our most precious natural resource, and any investment in our children is an investment in our future.

"I look out at your bright faces, and I see the promise of tomorrow, mingled with fond memories of the past. You might not believe it to look at me, but I was once your age, too."

This was the point at which Cheswick's media consultant had suggested creating a photo-op by making physical contact with one of the children. Cheswick bent over and reached out toward a towheaded boy in the front row. The boy showed as little emotion as the rest, but had the advantage of being within arm's reach. Cheswick ruffled his fingers through the boy's hair . . .

And screamed.

It took a moment for even Cheswick to realize that the

scream had come, not from the boy's mouth, but his own. Even so, however, there was no question why he was screaming. Cheswick recoiled in horror as, without warning, hundreds of cockroaches suddenly swarmed out from under the boy's hair and up the Senator's arm. He staggered back, flailing madly as he tried in vain to shake off the inch-long, brown monsters. But still they kept coming.

The insects were moving much too fast. As they sped along his body, Cheswick could see their hairy legs, their black eyes, and their quivering antennae. Cheswick's skin turned clammy with fear. He clawed at his jacket, hoping to rid himself of the vermin by throwing it away. But they were past his jacket and starting to reach his skin by now. It was far too late.

The living wave was growing in strength, too. The cockroaches continued to stream out endlessly from beneath the boy's hair. But now, they were coming from everywhere. Literally millions of roaches had started to pour toward Cheswick from the walls, the floor, and the ceiling tiles. They were crawling up his legs and dropping down from above.

Why wasn't anyone doing anything? Why weren't they helping him?

The camera crews were useless, staring at the Senator with puzzled expressions. And for their part, the children's faces didn't seem to register even the slightest bit of interest. They continued to watch Cheswick, but it wasn't a look that indicated there was anything wrong. In fact, their faces held the same blank look of passive disdain that they'd shown since the moment he arrived. Even the boy with the roaches in his hair had barely blinked.

Cheswick wanted to scream at them. He wanted to know what was wrong with them. He wanted to cry for help. But he couldn't. The Senator had clamped his mouth firmly shut when the roaches reached his chest, and was too afraid to open it now that he was swatting them away from his face. Keeping his lips pursed tightly together was helping to prevent the roaches from crawling inside, but they were starting toward his nose and ears.

All Cheswick could do was back away from the on-coming flood. He retreated as far as he could, until he felt himself bump up against the window. The roaches were coming from all sides now, sweeping toward him like a massive, living blanket. The past merged with the present as memories from the dumpster rushed through his tortured brain to mesh with the events of the moment. He was at once a 53-year-old man and nine-year-old boy, both victims of a terror that strained his heart to bursting. As the roaches flowed over his body, Cheswick took the only escape he could.

He hurled himself through the window.

Even as he plummeted seventeen stories to the street below, Cheswick beat furiously at the creatures that now covered virtually every inch of his body. The rushing wind tore some away, but his skin was alive now with the mass of chittering insects. He twisted and contorted his body every which way, but to no avail.

Cheswick was so consumed by the effort that he never even noticed when he hit the sidewalk.

Far above the cracked, bloody pavement, the youth center erupted with sound. A routine filler item had suddenly leaped forward to the front page.

"Jumped! That's right—jumped!"

"Bosnia? Forget Bosnia! Clear some space! You've gotta get this!"

"How should I know why? You want me to go after him and ask?!"

"Uh huh, get me a copywriter . . ."

". . . just came out of nowhere! All of a sudden, he goes into some kind of fit, and before you know it . . ."

"After falling, like, twenty floors?! Yeah, I'm pretty sure he's dead!"

"I dunno, it looked like DTs or something . . ."

"Killed himself! Right! As in 'dead!' "

"Yes, of course I'm getting pictures!"

Photographers were holding cell phones in one hand while they were snapping pictures with the other. Some were leaning out the window, capturing the pulpy remains of the former U.S. senator for posterity. Others were already on their way down the elevators and stairs to get a better shot.

The Senator's aide was in shock. All of the color had drained from his face, leaving him ashen and speechless as he was assaulted with a relentless barrage of questions and flash bulbs.

"Did you know the Senator was planning this?"

"Why did he do it?"

"Had he ever attempted suicide before?"

"Can you give me a statement?"

"Was he having marital problems?"

"Did he have a drug habit?"

"Was the Senator undergoing any kind of psychiatric treatment?"

"How are you feeling right now?"

The aide leaned back against the wall for support, his legs feeling much too weak to hold him. It was all he could do to stammer out most of an "I—I don't . . . know . . ."

In all the commotion, the only people who actually belonged in the youth center were all but forgotten. As chaos reigned all around them, the teacher quietly motioned for the children to get up. Gingerly avoiding the reporters rushing back and forth, she calmly escorted them away from the mob and toward the door.

The visitors to the center weren't in a frame of mind to notice subtleties. As a result, no one noticed the fact that the children's disinterested expressions still hadn't changed very much. Nor did they notice the teacher's small smile.

But that wasn't the strange thing.

The strange thing was that, from the moment the Senator arrived until the moment he struck the ground . . .

. . . no one had seen even a trace of a cockroach.

CHAPTER 2

Two months later . . .

The woman was a blur of motion, moving almost faster than the eye could follow. Originally, the odds seemed stacked against her, surrounded as she was by more than a dozen assailants, all of whom were female as well. But in moments, it was clear who truly had the upper hand.

The woman leaped up in the air, somersaulting past a pair of her astonished foes, and let herself fall to the floor, where she knocked their legs out from under them with a sweeping kick. In an eyeblink, she was back on her feet, meeting her next attacker with a rapid-fire series of jabs to the body and head. Before the attacker so much as hit the ground, she had already grabbed a staff from her assailant's hands, spun around, and used it to deflect the gleaming sword blade that slashed down toward her. Even as she bent one knee to absorb the impact, she planted the other foot smack in the middle of the swordswoman's torso, sending her staggering back as she whipped the staff around to strike the swordswoman (who no longer held the sword) in the side of the head.

"Whooooa . . . ," said Bobby.

"I have to apologize," Sarah whispered, in a hushed tone of awe.

"For what?" Bobby whispered back.

Sarah spoke without once taking her eyes from the scene of carnage before her. "When you and Grunge asked if we were up for this, I thought it was just another stupid guy thing. But the sheer level of mastery these women have developed. . . . Too bad Kat couldn't make it to see this. It's incredible."

"Mmmmm . . . catfight . . ." Grunge murmured. He leaned back in the dark with a blissful smile. A thin line of drool eased down his chin to splash on his chest.

Back up on the movie screen, another pair of attackers, wielding chains and an ornate battleaxe, were chasing the woman toward a blank wall. Without breaking stride, she leaped up at the wall. She used her momentum to literally run several steps up the wall before flipping back over and using her weight to put down her opponents with a double kick.

Only one of her assailants was left now. However, from the way that all of the action suddenly screeched to a halt, the quick cuts, and the fast zooms into tight close-ups on the two women's faces, it was clear that the last one was the most dangerous of all. The two of them stared at each other for a long moment, each one taking the other's measure. The woman breathed heavily from her exertion so far, while her final opponent looked cool.

Then, the silence was broken. With a pair of piercing screams, they ran toward the other and simultaneously took inhumanly long leaps through the air. They met in mid-flight, delivering and parrying a breathtaking hail-storm of blows before completing their trajectories and landing on the ground to carry on the battle at blinding speed.

"Check that out!" Roxy squealed, her body tense with excitement. "How do they *do* that, like in mid-air and stuff?"

Bobby shot her a sidelong glance. He raised an eyebrow and smirked. "Excuse me?" he said, taking another handful of popcorn. "Aren't you the one who's always messing around with gravity?"

"Well, sure," she replied, "but that's different. I mean, *this*. . . ." Roxy turned to Grunge, who was sitting on her other side, with his arm draped around her. "Y'know, sweetie?"

"That Michelle Yeoh is *hot*," Grunge said, his gaze fixated on the screen.

Roxy stiffened.

After about an hour or so, the lobby of the theater rang with laughter as the four friends spilled out of the matinee, jabbing at each other with mock-martial moves as they made their way through the lobby, toward the exit. Even Sarah, who was usually the most serious of the group by far, had allowed herself to get caught up in the moment, improvising catlike moves with a lithe grace.

"Beware the wrath of the Dragon Lotus! Haiii-ya!"

"Your wrath is as nothing before the teachings of the Golden Way!"

"Ha! With moves like that, dude, it's more like the 'Golden *No* Way!' "

"Hey, hey, hey! Let's remember who's the genuine martial arts master here!"

"Shyeah! Newsflash: Getting kicked out of a dojo for lack of discipline when you were ten does *not* make you a martial arts master!"

A skinny, acne-ridden usher, no older than the teenage patrons, watched the group and rolled his eyes. *It never fails*, he thought, shaking his head. *After every single show, it's always the same thing. There's always somebody who thinks he's the next Jackie Chan.* Well, at least this particular bunch seemed to be playing instead of looking for trouble. And at least they were heading for the door.

Not that he would have minded if the girls stuck around. The taller, graceful one was almost six feet tall and all curves. Her dark skin and the straight, jet black hair that reached down to her waist suggested that she was Latina or Native American or something. Whatever it was, it gave her an elegant "otherness" that the usher wouldn't have minded exploring for himself.

Her friend's looks were almost a total contrast, but she was equally cute in her own way. She was shorter and slender, with a relatively pale complexion. Her bangs were dyed pink to match the mini-skirt that barely covered her hips. In place of a blouse, she wore a frilly halter top that showed plenty of skin beneath her leather jacket. Fishnet stockings and go-go boots completed the outfit, giving the overall impression of a downtown girl who'd seen plenty of action. The usher figured he could do with a little of that action himself.

Of course, that wasn't to say that the usher had any realistic intention of approaching either of them. He hadn't tried asking a girl out since the humiliation that he still referred to, with a shudder, as "the Mindy Incident."

Besides, these girls were with a couple of guys already. Fairly intimidating guys, at that. One of them was tall and muscular, with close-cropped blonde hair and a small, matching tuft of blonde hair on his chin. As far as competing for the girls' attention was concerned, the blonde's matinee-idol looks put him way past the usher's league. All he could do was hope the guy was gay.

The last member of the quartet was intimidating, too, but in a totally different way. He was, by far, the shortest of the group, but at the same time, he was also the broadest by a considerable margin. Loud and unshaven, he gave the impression of being able to step out of the shower already grimy and just a little bit scuzzy. He was a mass of muscle, and he showed off his build by not wearing a shirt, despite the brisk winter weather outside. His jacket hung open, displaying a tattoo of a winged skull that was splashed across his chest.

Suddenly, the usher broke off his idle musings and froze, as his eyes locked with the blonde guy's. Immediately, he realized he'd been busted. Rule number one of avoiding trouble in New York City was to never, ever stare at anyone, and absolutely not to make eye contact. It wouldn't do any good to look away now, though. He'd already been caught, and if these guys were looking for trouble, he'd given them their opening.

The blonde guy held his gaze for a bit, his lips curled in a knowing smile as though he knew exactly what was on the usher's mind. Then, with a slight nod of acknowledgement, the blonde guy turned away. He and his friends tumbled out the door and into the crisp afternoon air, still laughing and sparring among themselves.

The usher breathed a sigh of relief. He went back to sweeping up stray kernels of popcorn from the floor.

"Ohmigawd! It's *freezing* out here!" Roxy grabbed the lapels of her leather jacket and pulled it close around her body.

"Well, duh," Bobby said with a grin. "It *is* December. Maybe the mini wasn't such a great idea after all, huh?"

Roxy stuck her tongue out at him. "Fashion demands sacrifice, pal. Besides, it's easy for you to say! Not all of us are walking radiators like you, y'know."

The snow had started to fall while they were watching the movie, and there was already about half an inch of the slushy, brown stuff coating the city streets. The tall buildings around them gave rise to a wind tunnel effect that intensified the chill wind that cut through them to the bone.

Just then, a passing cab sped by. It bounced through a nearby pothole, spraying their legs with the icy muck that had accumulated inside. Roxy's fishnets afforded little protection.

"Ewwwww!" she squealed. "I *hate* this city!"

Sarah zipped up her down parka with a shiver. "Well, I've got to side with Roxy on the weather thing," she said. "A lifetime in Arizona and La Jolla didn't exactly leave me loving the cold."

She thought for a moment. "Hey, 'walking radiator,' " Sarah added, "don't you think you can do something about this?"

Bobby shrugged. "Sure," he replied, "if you'll keep the snow off us."

"Deal."

Bobby started to raise his body temperature, careful not to go too high. Higher temperatures wouldn't do him any harm, but the gang was in civilian dress right now and the sidewalks were crammed with passers-by. Somehow, he suspected that transforming his body into a mass of living flame would probably blow their cover.

At the same time, Sarah concentrated, subtly manipulating the weather patterns around them. You'd have to look closely to spot the change, but even though the snow was still falling, not a single flake was landing on any of them. Fortunately, it wasn't likely that many people would be watching them all that closely. Many of them were keeping their heads down because of the snow. And besides, this was one time when the city's "no eye contact" rule worked in the group's favor.

"Mmmm . . .'wayyyy better. Toasty warm," Roxy said, rubbing her hands together. She called over to Grunge: "Hey, Grungie—come get in out of the cold!"

Grunge was standing some distance away, near the entrance to the theater. He was staring at a poster for the movie they had just seen.

"Yoo hoo," Roxy called again. "Earth to Grunge?"

Grunge jumped a bit, startled, as though he'd been off in a world of his own. He turned toward his friends with a leer. "Man," he said, "that Michelle Yeoh's a hottie! Did you see the way she was moving in there? All those tricks with flipping around and running up walls and all? Just imagine what she could do under . . . ahem . . . other circumstances, if you know what I mean . . ."

"Dude," Bobby replied, "we always know what you mean."

Grunge continued, undeterred. "Yup, yup, yup. Talk about your zero-gravity lovin'. Mm-hmm!"

Roxy gave Grunge a look that made the winter weather

pale by comparison. Bobby rubbed his eyes, looking pained. Sarah simply wasn't amused.

". . . What?" asked Grunge.

Roxy's eyes narrowed. "So you want gravity tricks, huh?"

"Uh oh," muttered Bobby.

"Well, maybe what you *really* need is a good, cold shower!"

Suddenly, the slushy snow hanging off of the marquee above Grunge doubled in weight, instantly becoming far too heavy to stay in place. Grunge shouted in surprise and indignation as the watery slop splattered over his head and shoulders, covering him in the dripping mess.

"Y'know, I don't think it's so cold after all," Roxy said, an edge in her voice. "I'll see you all at home." She spun on her heel and stormed off.

Sarah looked at Bobby with a resigned air that testified to the number of times they'd done this before. "I'll get her, you get him?"

"Yeah, okay."

Sarah hurried off after Roxy. "Roxanne! Wait up!"

Bobby casually strolled slowly over to where Grunge stood, still dripping wet.

"What?" said Grunge, honestly baffled.

Bobby sighed. He draped an arm around his best friend's shoulder. "Grunge-man," he said, "you've got a lot to learn about women."

Grunge looked genuinely surprised, and more than a little offended. "Whatchoo talkin' 'bout, Willis? I know plenty about women! Hey, I read *Penthouse Letters* every month. Even wrote a couple . . ."

Bobby sighed again. "Listen, you and Roxy've been going out for, what, a month or two now?"

"Yeah."

"And how do you feel about her?"

"How do you think I feel? I dig her. She's my swee-tie."

"And she digs you."

"Damn skippy. I'm the man."

"Well, 'the man,' how do you think it makes Roxy feel when she hears you going on and on about Michelle Yeoh?"

Grunge pondered that for a minute. He scratched his head in confusion. "But I thought chicks are always after us to be honest. Share our feelings, and all that bull. So I was just being honest about my feelings about Michelle Yeoh . . ."

Bobby shook his head. "Dude, there's honest, and there's honest. You've got to choose your subject matter a little better. You want to talk about your love of kittens and puppy dogs, that's cool. But they don't want to hear about you having the hots for somebody else."

Grunge nodded sagely, taking it all in. "Guess that figures."

"Guess so."

"Guess I should go apologize, huh?"

"Guess you're catching on."

By the time Bobby finished talking with Grunge, Sarah had already caught up with Roxy. The two of them were standing halfway down the block, having a conversation of their own.

". . . I mean, it's not like I don't know how he is. I know how he is. I knew that before we started going out," Roxy was saying. She paused for a moment while she lit a cigarette and inhaled deeply. She held the smoke in her lungs for a long moment, then released it all at once. The swirling tendrils of smoke mixed with the vapor from her breath in the chill air.

"It's just . . ." Roxy looked around as though searching the buildings around her for the words she needed. "Well, it's bad enough when it's some eight-foot-tall supermodel with pneumatic boobs bigger than her head. At least then I know what's missing about me."

"Roxanne, there's nothing missing about you . . ."

"Oh, get real. 'You've got a good heart, and that's all

21

that matters, and besides, you're cute as a button, blah blah blah.' Look, I know I'm not built like you, and I'm sure not built like Kat. And it's cool. I accept that.

"But Michelle Yeoh? Michelle freakin' Yeoh?! She's, like, *my* size! If he starts liking *her* better than me, then, well, what's up with that? What am I supposed to do about it?"

Sarah opened her mouth to answer. But before she could say anything, Grunge came running up to join them. Bobby followed behind. "Hey, Rox! Hey! Hold up!"

Grunge came to a stop beside Roxy. She turned away.

"C'mon, baby, don't be like that," he coaxed. "I'm dirt. I'm pond scum. I'm a horn dog who hasn't thought with his brain since puberty."

"I don't believe you're hearing me disagree."

"But I'm sorry, okay? I'm really, really sorry. That stuff doesn't mean anything. My mouth just works faster than my brain sometimes. I didn't mean to hurt your feelings or anything. Y'know? I just get like that around hot chicks."

"Oh, good. It makes me feel soooo much better knowing that you didn't do it on purpose. You just get like that around *hot* chicks."

"C'mon, I'm trying here, okay? Just cut me a little slack. You mean a lot to me."

Roxy didn't say anything.

"There's gotta be a way I can prove I'm serious about this . . ." Grunge said.

He thought for a second, then snapped his fingers. "I know! I know how I can prove it to you!"

He raised his hand solemnly—or as solemnly as he could. "From now on, I, Percival Edmund Chang, will never talk about another woman, or sex, or anything like that in front of you again!"

The others stared at him in stunned silence.

Then they burst into howls of laughter that left them barely able to stand.

"What?" Grunge asked. "What's the joke?"

Roxy wiped the tears of laughter from her eyes. "Oh, Grunge, sweetie, that's really sweet of you. Really. But . . ." She broke off the sentence as another fit of laughter seized her.

Grunge looked around at the hysterical trio, a little offended. "What, you don't think I can do it?"

Bobby stopped coughing barely long enough to catch his breath. "Shyeah. Dude, no offense, but you couldn't stop talking about sex long enough to microwave popcorn!"

"No, huh? Shows what *you* know! If I put my mind to something, then it's a done deal! I'm all about will power! I'm the very model of will power! I'm the mack daddy of will power!"

The only response was a gale of laughter that dwarfed the first one.

"O . . . . okay," Bobby said, struggling to get himself back under control. "I'll tell you what. I'll . . ." He fought off a giggle. "I'll bet you a hundred bucks . . . that you . . . that you can't go a whole week . . . without talking about sex."

Grunge shook his hand with a slightly-too-firm grip. "Money in the bank, dude. You're on!"

Sarah wheezed and clutched her aching stomach. "Oh, now I *really* wish Kat was here. She shouldn't miss this." She took a deep breath. "Where is Kat, anyway?"

"Don't know," Roxy replied, snuggling back up against her boyfriend. "All she said was she had stuff to do."

In another part of the city, Caitlin Fairchild made her way through the crowded streets, heading nowhere in particular. Kat wore only a light jacket over her turtleneck and jeans, but she barely noticed the cold or the snow around her. Part of the reason was her super-tough skin that made her impervious to all sorts of things, not the least of which was the cold. Mostly, though, it was because she was lost in thought.

Apart from the cold, Kat also barely noticed the stares she got from virtually every man she passed. Only a couple of years ago, Kat had been a mousy teenager with glasses who rarely elicited a second glance from the males on campus. But that was before she'd gone gen-active and transformed into a six-foot-three amazon with striking red hair and a figure that made Pamela Anderson look like Olive Oyl. Since the big change, she'd grown so accustomed to the stares of astonishment and naked lust that they just became part of the baggage that came with the deal.

In fact, Kat had been spending a lot of time lately thinking about those days before her time with Gen[13]. Back in the day, Kat had been a promising student at Princeton University. A's didn't come easy at Princeton, but that didn't stop her from earning more than her share. She'd majored in computer science back then, and dreamt of a bright future in which she'd dazzle the world with new and daring innovations that would make people's lives better.

And if she earned a small fortune along the way, well, that wouldn't be so bad either.

However, everything changed one night toward the end of Kat's sophomore year, when she was awakened by a late-night knock on the door of her dorm room. It was a team of men in dark suits, agents of the National Security Committee. They'd come to tell her that she'd been accepted for an internship connected to a highly classified government program for unusually talented young people.

In retrospect, Kat should have realized that something was funny when they told her that she would have to leave school that same night to be processed into the program. At the time, though, it was all happening so fast, and she was so grateful and flattered to be chosen, that she never stopped to think about it.

By dawn, Kat found herself in a high-tech facility in the heart of Death Valley. The place was run by a covert group called International Operations, or I.O. for short. It was quite a change from Princeton, what with its halls lined with electronics and guards dressed up in sophisticated cybernetic armor.

It was here that Kat would meet the four people who would soon become her closest friends:

Sarah Rainmaker, a full-blooded Apache with a self-righteous passion for causes ranging from women's rights to saving the environment to helping the homeless.

Bobby Lane, who'd been bounced from foster home to foster home for as long as he could remember. The experience had left Bobby bitter and angry in those days, but even back then, his more sensitive side occasionally peeked through in his love of music.

Roxanne Spaulding, a chain-smoking party girl whose in-your-face attitude masked a genuine sweetness underneath.

And Grunge, who was . . . well, Grunge.

The days at I.O. quickly blurred into an endless series of mental and physical tests that went far beyond anything Kat had ever experienced in college. After two years at an Ivy League school, Kat was used to pencil-and-paper exams and computer assignments that challenged her mental abilities. But here, she also found herself pumping iron and running on treadmills—not to mention being poked and prodded every which way by mechanical sensors built into the glass walls of what looked like giant test tubes while she was suspended inside, wearing nothing but an embarrassed expression. There were times when Kat felt more like a lab rat than a "talented young person."

Of course, Kat hadn't known the real reason why she and the others had been selected, any more than she knew the real purpose of the program. She didn't know that she was part of the thirteenth generation of the Genesis Project, whose hidden agenda was to create super-powered operatives under the control of Ivana Baiul, the ruthless leader of I.O.'s Sci-Tech division. She didn't know that, like her new friends, she'd been chosen because her father was one of the successes of the twelfth generation of the program—a member of a covert, super-powered strike force that was given the code name Team 7. Most important, she didn't know about the drugs that were being slipped into her food at every meal, or the treatments that were being administered while she was "under examination" in the tubes. All of them added up to a regimen that was designed to activate her latent powers . . . if they didn't kill her first.

In fact, Kat and her friends were far from the only test subjects at the facility. There were at least a half-dozen other groups of teens who were undergoing the same brutal regimen of tests they were. Over the weeks they spent training, however, each of the other groups would either wash out of the program or disappear.

That destiny wasn't in the cards for Kat, though. She still held vivid memories of the night when her gen-factor kicked in. The nausea. The headaches that wouldn't go away and just kept getting worse. And then, the white-hot pain that coursed through every inch of her frame. It felt like her body was tearing itself apart—and, in a sense, it was. The very strands of her DNA ripped apart and reformed as Kat's body expanded and morphed until she couldn't even recognize herself anymore. She gained nearly a foot in height, not to mention enhanced speed and the strength and durability of a small tank.

The others had proven to be gen-active as well. Bobby took on the code name "Burnout" to reflect his newfound ability to hurl blasts of fiery plasma and transform parts of his own body into living flame. Sarah found herself able to manipulate Earth's natural elements, while Roxy (newly christened "Freefall") discovered her own ability to control gravity, making things either super-heavy or super-light. Grunge's power was the most diverse, allowing him to mimic the properties and molecular structure of any object he touched. Sarah and Kat decided to keep their own surnames, Rainmaker and Fairchild, as their code names. And as for Grunge, well, no one could come up with anything more appropriate to call him than "Grunge."

They weren't the first of Gen^{13} to go gen-active. That honor belonged to a psychotic brother-sister team known as Threshold and Bliss. The homicidal duo became Ivana's personal pets long before the rest of them had even shown up on the scene. But Kat and her friends were the ones to adopt the name "Gen^{13}" as their own.

Yet, Kat reflected, they'd still probably be pawns of I.O. today if it wasn't for the intervention of John Lynch. Lynch had been the head of I.O.'s Operations section, and before that, he'd served alongside the kids' parents as part of Team 7. He didn't like what was going on at I.O., and when his conscience refused to let him look the other way, he decided to do something about it. Lynch's career with the agency came to an abrupt end when he helped Gen^{13} bust out of the I.O. compound and took in the young fugitives to teach them how to use their new powers and stay alive.

It wasn't until much later that the team learned that Lynch also had another reason for helping them escape:

Bobby was his son.

All of them had come a long way since then, in a deceptively short period of time. Gen^{13} had fought any number of super-powered menaces and would-be rulers of the world, and they'd always come out on top. Their days on the run were over; I.O. was ancient history now, disbanded amid scandal that even the shadowy organization's best "public information specialists" couldn't spin their way out of.

But it wasn't all good news. The gang's dream house in Southern California had been blasted into so much kindling along the way. That was what had given them the push to come east and start over again, here in New York City.

And Kat had come through all of it before she even turned twenty.

Kat looked back at the last year or so of her life, and marvelled at the unexpected turns it had taken. Heaven knows, it wasn't what she had planned. If it were possible for someone to go back in time and tell her younger, bespectacled self what lay in store, she'd have thought the oracle was crazy. *But then again*, she thought, *I guess things don't always turn out like we plan.*

It wasn't that Kat regretted what had become of her life, exactly. After all, not everyone can say that they've saved the world more times than they can count on their fingers. She couldn't even remember the faces of everyone whose life she had saved at one time or another. Fate had handed Kat a rare opportunity, and she was grateful for the chance to live up to it.

Plus, there were personal benefits, too. Her Gen[13] teammates were the closest friends she'd ever had in her life. They'd become like family—especially when it turned out that Roxy was really Kat's half-sister. If truth be told, the band of friends was tighter than a lot of "real" families. Every one of them was dearer to her than anything, and she wouldn't trade that for the world.

It was just that Kat never expected to wind up with her teammates as her *only* friends. Sure, the stuff she was doing was vital in a reactive kind of way, stopping danger before it could claim innocent lives. Someone had to be there to right the wrongs, and sail in at blinding speed . . .

(Kat smiled despite herself. The phrasing made her sound like Underdog. *"When in this world the headlines read/Of those whose hearts are filled with greed. . . ."* Gee, she hadn't watched that show since she was eight. How on Earth did she remember the song?)

But that's just dealing with the stuff that's already happened, she thought, turning her mind back to the matter at hand. *What about the future?*

What about my *future?*

Was Kat going to wind up spending the rest of her life in a skintight outfit, showing off her legs while trashing the master villain of the week?

That was the path Mister Lynch had chosen for himself. The scars on his face and the cybernetic, mechanical eye that he wore in place of his real one bore witness to an endless series of battles. For all intents and purposes, those battles constituted the sum total of Lynch's adult life.

Kat could imagine herself still doing this at age fifty, her hair showing touches of gray and the costume altered to allow for her sagging, middle-age spread. It wasn't a picture that held a whole lot of appeal.

I need a life, she thought.

Suddenly, Kat was jarred out of her reverie. A shout came from nearby, along with the unmistakable sound of a fist striking flesh.

Without so much as a second thought, Kat took off running. She followed the sounds into an alley, where she found a gang of four street punks in matching fatigue jackets and camouflage pants. The four were hovering like vultures around a young man in an overcoat and a conservative business suit. The young man was half-sitting, half-lying on the ground as one of the punks pawed through the pockets of his coat. A bruise was already forming on the side of the victim's face.

Kat dropped her coat to the ground, so it wouldn't restrict her movement, and struck a pose. Even in civilian clothes, she cut an imposing figure. "Hold it right there!" she commanded.

The punks spun at the sound of her voice, simultaneously reaching under their coats for the weapons that were hidden there. They froze at the sight of her, with looks of disbelief on their faces.

"What the hell . . . ?"

"Oh, mama . . ."

The four punks stopped reaching for the weapons. Slowly, each of them smiled. One even licked his lips.

I can't believe you just did that, Kat thought.

The nearest punk strutted over toward her in a way that he probably thought was seductive. He gave a low whistle as he eyed her from top to bottom. "Sweet thing," he said, "you just chill a minute. Soon as we're done with that loser over there, then you and us, we'll have us a real par—"

The rest of the sentence died in a strangled "urk" as Kat grabbed the front of his coat and lifted him up, effortlessly, above her head. With one hand, Kat hurled him through the air to smash into the wall.

The far wall.

At the end of the alley.

A good fifty feet away.

All of a sudden, the other punks weren't smiling anymore. "Bust a cap in her!" one of them yelled.

In a flash, the three produced handguns as if from nowhere. They held the guns out at arm's length, turned sideways, and opened fire on Kat.

Kat shook her head. It wasn't so much at the futility of the hail of bullets, which hurt as they bounced off her but posed about as much of a threat as the flakes of snow that continued to fall from the sky. The thing Kat was reacting to was the amateurish way they handled their weapons. *They're not even using the sights*, she thought. Either they were going for image over accuracy, or they'd seen too many movies. If Mister Lynch had been their instructor, he would have had their heads.

The carnage that followed was mercifully brief. In a matter of minutes, the punks lay broken and bleeding on the ground. The sound of distant sirens reached Kat's ears, signalling her that it was time to go.

But before she could leave, she had to check on the victim.

She bent down over the young man in the suit. "Are you okay?" she asked.

"Oh, yeah. Absolutely," he said. A dreamy smile crossed his swollen face as she helped him to his feet. "You—you were amazing! The way you took those guys out. . . ."

"It was nothing."

"Well, it was something to me! You've got to let me

repay you somehow. I know—dinner! Let me take you to dinner tonight."

"That's really not necessary."

"What do you mean, not necessary? I insist! It's the least I can do. For my female knight in shining armor."

Kat could feel the blush spreading in her cheeks.

"A little lobster," he coaxed. "Or maybe a filet mignon."

Kat's resolve was starting to crack.

"A little dancing, a nice bottle of wine . . ."

It did sound tempting.

"And then, afterwards, a romantic evening at my place. A little candlelight, some baby oil . . ."

"What?!"

A moment later, Kat picked up her coat and left the alley.

From his position upside down in the trash can, the guy in the suit called after her. "I'm in the book!" he yelled. "Call me!"

There has got *to be more to life than this* . . . , Kat thought.

CHAPTER 3

The Congressional aide knocked softly on the door before entering. "Representative Sturmer?" she whispered. Tentatively, the aide held up five fingers and said, half in a whisper and half in mime, "Five minutes until the committee meeting."

Sturmer nodded and raised a hand to signal the aide to wait. The telephone receiver never left her ear. ". . . Okay. What did she say then?" Sturmer said into the phone. There was a pause as she listened to the person on the other end of the line. "Uh-huh. Well, Taleisha, she *is* your mother . . ."

A pause. "I know. I know you're not . . ."

Another pause. "Absolutely. You're absolutely right. But you have to see it from her side, too. She loves you. And she's concerned about you . . .

"Well, maybe that's what you need to tell *her*. But try to remember to listen, too, okay? . . .

"Yes, okay. Now, let's get back to business. Did you get the materials I sent you for the civics project? . . .

"Good. See what you can do with all of that, and if you have any questions, give me a call. Okay? . . .

"Okay, I will. I have to go to a meeting now. I'll talk to you soon, okay? And take it easy on your mom. . . .

"Okay. Goodbye now, dear."

Sturmer replaced the receiver in its cradle. She exhaled sharply and smiled at the aide as she replaced the bulky gold earring that she had removed while talking on the phone. "Whooof!" she said. "I'm sorry about that, but some things take priority.

"Come, let's get to the meeting. You can brief me on the way."

The Honorable Charlene Sturmer had come of age in the mid-1960s. Like so many of her contemporaries, she had felt a burning desire to change what was wrong with American society. Yet, unlike so many of her contemporaries, she didn't see the point in trying to tear down the institutions of the Establishment. Instead, she believed that she could have a much greater impact in the long run by lending her efforts toward preserving the things that did work and improving the things that didn't. Instead of trying to break down the walls from the outside, she imagined that it would be easier to try to change things from the inside.

However, she soon learned that before she could work from the inside, she'd first have to get through the door. And getting through the door proved to be anything but easy. These were the days before the women's movement and sex discrimination suits. In government circles—and too many others—women still were seen as little more than potential secretaries and decorations. She worked her butt off for months, going door to door to campaign personally for a seat on the local city council. And even after she landed the seat, she found her opinions ignored by a chauvinistic, patronizing mayor. Once, he'd gone so far as to respond to Sturmer's revolutionary plan for streamlining the entire city budget by literally patting her on the head.

Despite it all, though, Charlene Sturmer hadn't been raised to be a quitter. She worked long and hard for years, doing her level best to fight for the people she represented.

Her big break came when she was offered a shot at running for lieutenant governor under Governor Zachary Yale—the first time a woman would be running for the office. Sturmer had no illusions about the reason why the higher-ups in the party had picked her; from their perspective, it was a political move, motivated by a desire to capture the female vote.

But whatever motives anyone else might have had, Yale didn't care about Sturmer's gender. He studied her record and was impressed by what he saw. If she was willing to work, then he was willing to listen. At first, Sturmer smiled and nodded, shrugging his words off as typical political rhetoric. Soon, though, she came to realize that he meant every word of it.

Under Yale's tutelage, Sturmer blossomed. She'd already read all the books, and learned the rules and regulations. But with Yale as her mentor, she soon learned how to negotiate the unwritten rules as well.

It took years of sweat and toil, but little by little, Sturmer fought her way up the ladder to make a name for herself. And now, here she was, thirty-five years later, on Capitol Hill. She'd grown into an accomplished legislator and a valued member of the House Ways and Means Committee, a driving force in determining exactly how the United States government spent its money each year. Sturmer's dogged determination and commitment to her principles had won her the respect of even those colleagues who constantly disagreed with her.

Still, through it all, Sturmer had never forgotten her roots. She never forgot how hard the road had been, or how much help she'd needed from others in order to get over the hurdles. That was why she devoted so much of her free time to working as a volunteer mentor for teenage girls, doing what she could to help them succeed in school and their future goals. She'd lost count of just how many girls like Taleisha she'd helped over the years, but many of them still filled her mailbox to bursting with holiday cards on a regular basis. She cherished the relationships she had built with these girls, and while she didn't know where all of them were today, she could still see every single one of their young faces in her mind's eye.

Sturmer grabbed her purse and a leather-bound notebook from her desk as she walked to the door. The aide was already consulting her own notes to bring Sturmer up to speed. "Today's agenda leads off with a revised proposal for HR#22-571." She handed Sturmer a thick file of papers and followed her into the hall, past the uniformed guards who were stationed at regular intervals.

"Which one is that?" Sturmer asked.

"The allocations for satellite-guided missile development."

Sturmer made a face. "That nonsense again?"

"The contractor is one of Representative Zwiren's constituents."

"Oh, right." Sturmer flipped through the hefty document as she walked. "Does this revision make any more sense than the last one?"

"I'm afraid not."

"That's not much of a surprise, I suppose. Well, let's see what sort of case the old windbag makes this time."

"And then, after that . . ."

"Never mind the 'after that,' Maggie. You can throw out the rest of the agenda. This Zwiren thing's going to take a while."

"Will you want me to bring you some coffee?"

Sturmer grinned. "Lots of it, thanks."

As they turned the corner, Sturmer stopped at the sound of a quiet voice off to her side. "Representative Sturmer . . . ?"

She turned to see a slim, twelve-year-old girl standing there. The girl had long, dark hair and would have been quite pretty, if it weren't for the blank, impassive expression on her face. *It must be nerves, the poor dear,* Sturmer thought.

Sturmer bent down toward her with a warm smile. "Yes, that's right, dear. I'm Representative Sturmer. What's your name?"

The aide tapped Sturmer on the shoulder from behind. "Um, the meeting . . ."

Sturmer waved the reminder away with a dismissive gesture. "It's just a roomful of stuffy politicians. They can wait a few minutes. Some things take priority."

She turned back to the girl. "Now, what can I do for—?"

The girl's hand lashed out to clutch Sturmer's throat. In less time than it took to tell it, she crushed Sturmer's windpipe between her fingers.

Representative Charlene Sturmer fell to the floor, dead.

The aide stared, wide-eyed, then screamed.

From either side of the hall, a pair of armed guards came charging toward the scene, their rifles drawn. The closer one ordered the girl to halt. Yet, even as he raised his rifle, he knew that, deep down, he couldn't quite imagine shooting a twelve-year-old girl.

That was his mistake.

With blinding speed, the girl grabbed the barrel of his rifle and yanked it from his grip. She broke his arm in three places before he could react.

That was all the second guard had to see. Disregarding every regulation against discharging firearms in public places, he stopped outside of arm's reach, quickly took aim, and opened fire.

At least three of his bullets hit her dead center. He was sure of it.

But they didn't seem to have any effect.

Calmly, the girl picked up the first guard's fallen rifle. With one hand, she flung it at the second guard. The stock caught him right between the eyes, sending him flying off his feet. He was out cold before either his body or the rifle could hit the ground.

The aide cowered in terror against the opposite wall. Who *was* this girl? *What* was she?!

In fact, though, there was no longer anything to fear. The girl had already done what she came to do.

A second girl, similar in age but with short, curly hair, stepped out of a doorway to join the first. "We weren't supposed to engage the guards," she said. "Time to withdraw."

The first one nodded.

The second girl closed her eyes. The air beside them started to shimmer. The pair stepped purposefully toward the effect, and in the blink of an eye, they were gone without a trace. Only the bedlam that they left behind remained as proof that they had been there at all.

The whole thing had taken only a matter of minutes. With startling efficiency, two twelve-year-old girls had invaded one of the most secure areas in the country. They had overcome a pair of highly trained guards. They had committed cold-blooded murder.

And they had done it all without a single change of their impassive expressions.

The front office of the employment agency was a sea of noise. Between the ringing phones, the clicking of fingers on keyboards, the employment counselors pitching clients to potential employers, and the hopeful souls laying out their dreams of the future, it was hard for the people inside to hear themselves think:

"What kind of experience do you have?"

"Yes, I've got a terrific candidate sitting right here. I think you'll be very happy with her."

"I understand. Thanks anyway."

"Oh, sure! I see it now. So what you're saying is that maybe I could *start* with accounting, and then sort of ease my way gradually over toward lion tamer . . . ?"

The ongoing din wasn't uncommon at the agency. If anything, it simply signalled business as usual. It was far more uncommon when, a moment later, the noise came to an abrupt halt and an awestruck silence blanketed the room. One by one, all heads turned when Kat walked tentatively in through the door.

For a second, Kat worried that it might have been because of the bullet holes in her sweater. But a quick glance confirmed that they weren't visible; she'd had the foresight to keep her jacket zipped up to conceal them. After all, Kat figured, an outfit riddled with bullet holes might not make the best first impression.

No, Kat concluded that the reason was a much more familiar one. Even without bullet holes, Kat had grown used to the fact that she had a hard time blending into a crowd.

Screwing up her courage, Kat strode through the room. She tried to distract herself from the stares by focusing her attention on the room and its furnishings instead. The walls were a faded off-white, the desks and file cabinets were the standard sort of metallic black and gray that were typical of almost every office Kat had visited since her days in elementary school. (*Hmm*, Kat thought, reading the metal tag on the front of a desk as though it was deeply important. *"Ridgeway and Company, Akron, Ohio."*) Her feet followed along well-worn scuff marks in the linoleum that hinted at the many years' worth of people who'd gone before.

Kat headed for one of the few desks where the guest chair beside the desk wasn't already filled. A heavyset, middle-aged woman in horn-rimmed glasses sat behind the desk. Her fingers were still on the keyboard that she'd been using before Kat came through the door. The nameplate on the desk proclaimed her name as Rhoda Mickel.

Kat stood in front of the desk, her hands clasped together. She tried a nervous smile.

"Hi," said Kat.

"Yes?"

"I'd, uh . . . I'd like to find a job."

Ms. Mickel peered over the frame of her glasses and eyed Kat skeptically. Kat shifted her weight from foot to foot.

"Sorry," Ms. Mickel said, "this isn't a modelling agency." She turned her attention back to the computer and started to type.

Kat was dumbstruck. "But—but that's exactly the point!" she said. She leaned forward with an earnest look on her face. "I'm tired of people judging me by how I look. It's like everyone I meet out there is only looking at the surface, and not at the person underneath. I get too much of that already.

"I don't want the kind of job that comes because of how I look. I want the kind of job that comes because of who I am."

Ms. Mickel kept on typing. "Really," she said without looking up.

"Really," Kat replied.

Ms. Mickel pursed her lips, then swiveled back around in her chair to face Kat. "So let me see if I understand this. You're upset because you have a serious problem. There are just too many people out there who are attracted to your looks."

"Well, yes."

"Poor baby." Ms. Mickel went back to her typing.

Now, Kat was starting to get annoyed. "Look," she said, "I don't know what your problem is—"

"Oh, I don't have a problem. I just have trouble mustering up a lot of sympathy for a Barbie doll whose big complaint is that she's too gorgeous."

" 'Barbie doll?!' I was pulling down A's when I was at Princeton!"

"My mistake," said Ms. Mickel. But her dry tone suggested that she was still unimpressed.

"Why do you resent me so much? Because I'm pretty?" Kat said.

"Listen, sweetheart, I've been doing this for a long time. I've seen your type before. You start out all committed to working your way up the ladder. But then, when you realize that really means *working* your way up, it loses its appeal. So you start looking for the faster track." Without meaning to, she glanced over at the slim, blonde woman who was coming out of the manager's office. "You start batting your long eyelashes and passing over the less beautiful people who really deserve it!"

"You know, there are laws about discriminating against people because of how they look . . ."

41

Ms. Mickel shrugged. "Sue me. Does this place *look* like it has a huge bank account?"

"This is so unfair!" Kat exclaimed. "You don't know me! You don't know anything about me!"

"Oh?"

"I'm sorry if you've had bad experiences with those kinds of people before. But don't you see what you're doing? You're doing the exact same thing they do. You're holding me back because of my looks!"

Ms. Mickel raised her eyebrows at that one. Her fingers paused, then left the keyboard. Ms. Mickel sat back in her chair and looked up at Kat, clearly mulling the point over.

Finally, she spoke. "You really mean it, don't you?"

"Yes."

Ms. Mickel nodded slowly. She gestured toward her guest chair. "Sorry," she said. "I shouldn't have jumped to conclusions. It's been a bad day. Why don't you take a seat, and we'll see what we can do for you."

Kat's smile lit up her entire face. Somehow, this victory felt better than beating a hundred super-villains. She thanked Ms. Mickel and sat.

Ms. Mickel reached into her drawer and pulled out a pen and a pad. "Name?"

"Caitlin Fairchild."

Ms. Mickel started to write. "C-A-I-T . . ."

"L-I-N, yes."

"May I take a look at your resumé?"

Kat shook her head. "I, um, haven't put one together yet."

"Mmm, all right. Well, you mentioned Princeton. What sort of degree do you have? Bachelors? Masters?"

"Um, none, really. I did about two years of course work in computer science, but I never finished."

"So, are you currently employed?"

"No. Well, yes. I guess. Freelance, sort of."

" 'Freelance, sort of.' "

"Yes."

The corner of Ms. Mickel's mouth turned down with

a sardonic look. "You're not making this any easier, you know."

Kat gave a small, sheepish shrug. It made her look like the largest little girl on Earth.

Despite herself, Ms. Mickel smiled. "All right, let's see what we've got for you." She picked up one of the piles of paper from her desk and started to page through it. "Oh! Here we go! This one's perfect for you!"

Kat's heart leapt in her chest. "What is it?"

"There's an opening for lady wrestlers. How are you with hot mud?"

Kat's jaw dropped in disbelief.

"Just kidding," Ms. Mickel said with a wink. "Let's see what we can find in the way of entry-level computer jobs . . ."

The semi-nude couple writhed and intertwined across the tabletop. The scene dissolved into a series of passionate kisses and darting tongues, as they twisted their bodies in ways that seemed to defy the limits of human anatomy.

It was a miracle that no one else happened to come into the pizza shop.

"Her food's *gotta* be burning by now," Bobby said. "What did she order? A calzone?"

Sarah shook her head. "Pizza," she replied. She took on a breathy tone as she grinned and added, "With *everything* . . ."

"Golly, Grunge," Roxy said, shaking and shimmying around the room to the bump and grind music that pulsed through the moaning. "I never knew these 'special interest' videos of yours could be so entertaining. No wonder it's all you do all the time."

Grunge clasped a pair of throw pillows to his ears and kept his eyes clamped shut. "I'm not listening! I'm not listening! La la la la—I'm not listening!"

The gang was home now, sprawled across the plush, L-shaped sofa in their lavish penthouse suite at the Omni Seasons. Bobby reclined lazily in the corner of the L, and regarded his friend through half-closed eyes. "Something wrong, Gee? Not up for a little porn?" He gasped in mock horror. "Oh! The bet! This must make it real hard for you, huh? How insensitive of me."

With a grin, Bobby shot a glance at the television. "Oh, wait—here's a good part." He pointed the remote control at the screen and scanned back a few seconds to replay the scene. The woman was spanking the clerk with the paddle he used to make pizza.

All Grunge could do was voice a strangled cry.

Just then, the front door burst open. The team started to jump to their feet, instantly alert and ready to defend themselves against any possible attack. Then, they relaxed again as Kat literally danced into the apartment. She was singing to herself and virtually walking on air. Kat leaped and twirled around her friends, leaving them amused and curious.

"Geez," Roxy said, wide-eyed. "What's up with you, sis?"

Grunge gave a knowing look. "Looks like someone got herself a little—"

"A little *what*?" Bobby asked hastily.

Grunge caught himself. "Um . . . piece of paper. Kat's got a little piece of paper. In her hand, there."

"Grunge, my perceptive friend, you are so right!" Kat could hardly contain her excitement as she held up the paper that she carried. "I do indeed have a piece of paper in my hand. And do you know what's *on* this wonderful, little piece of paper?"

"Next week's lottery number?" Sarah said with a bemused smile.

Kat pretended not to hear her. She carefully opened the paper. "On this paper is a schedule of interviews. For *me*. For tomorrow."

"You're being interviewed?" Bobby asked.

"Like, on TV?" said Roxy.

"Or in *Play*—," said Grunge.

"What's that?" Bobby asked him.

"Um . . . in a magazine?" said Grunge. "One that doesn't have any pictures?"

Kat waved off the guesses with the back of her hand. "No, no, not that kind of interview," she said. "This is much better. So much better. I'm being interviewed—

"—for a *job!*"

Four pairs of eyes grew as wide as saucers. Kat beamed. For the longest time, no one spoke. Then, all four of her friends responded at once:

"A JOB?!"

Grinning widely, Kat nodded over and over. "Yes! A job! Can you believe it? Isn't it great?"

"Are you *nuts*?!" Roxy replied.

Grunge spread his arms wide and gestured around them. "What would you want a job for? Look around! We're already livin' large!"

It was true that the luxury apartment was something that most New Yorkers—who were used to paying four-figure rents each month for a single room the size of a closet—would kill for. The suite took up two floors of the posh building, and covered enough space to provide private bedrooms for each of the team, a study for Lynch, and even a small workout room. The sunken living room alone was three times the size of Kat's old dorm room at college, with a fully stocked bar and a picture window that spanned most of one wall to display a spectacular view of the city.

But that wasn't what was foremost in Kat's mind right now. And even if the others didn't see that, Sarah did. She stepped between Kat and the rest of the group. "Back off, you guys! She's not doing it for the money. There's more to life than fancy apartments." She turned to Kat. "Right?"

"Right."

Kat had known that, out of everyone, Sarah would understand. That was why, each week, Sarah spent several hours volunteering at a homeless shelter downtown.

Roxy stared up at Kat, her eyes starting to fill. "You

mean you . . . you're gonna just, like, split? After all this time, you'd just up and leave . . . um, the team?"

Kat flashed her a reassuring smile. "No way, silly! I'd never leave you guys. We do some important stuff here.

"Besides," she added, putting her arm around Roxy and giving her a squeeze that nearly cracked a rib, "after nineteen years, I finally found my sister. Do you think I'd let you slip away now?"

Roxy managed to choke out a feeble "Thanks . . ." as the one-armed hug forced the air from her lungs.

Kat let go and went back to addressing the group as a whole. "But," she said, "I've got an obligation to myself, too. I have to do something about this. I can't just ignore my own needs."

"Hey, while you're at it, you can always pay some attention to *my* nee—," Grunge joked. Then he looked at Bobby. ". . . Never mind."

Bobby smirked at Grunge, enjoying his friend's discomfort. But his smile faded and his face turned sincere when he spoke to Kat. "We get it, Kat. If this is what you need, it's cool. You know we'll always be behind you, no matter what."

Kat smiled with relief. "Thanks."

"But," Bobby continued, "even if you've got us on board, you're still going to have a mega-problem here."

Sarah looked serious as she nodded in agreement. She knew full well what Bobby was talking about. "Lynch isn't going to like this."

The team's mentor had been away for the past few days. He hadn't said where he was going. But his presence was still very much with them.

"I know," Kat said. "That's why you've got to help me out. I need to find some way to break it to him, so that—"

Kat stopped talking as soon as she heard the familiar, deep voice behind her. "I believe it's already broken," said the voice.

Kat looked up to see Lynch standing in the open front

door. He was still wearing his coat and holding a leather carry-on bag. There was no way to know just how long he'd been standing there.

Dressed in a jet black shirt and trousers, Lynch cut a commanding figure. He was well into middle age, but his body was as taut and muscular as it had been twenty years earlier. His mutton chops and widow's peak accentuated the sharp angles of his scarred face.

As a general rule, Lynch rarely smiled. But even by his own standards, he didn't look happy.

Lynch turned to the others. "Would you excuse us, please? Caitlin and I need to talk."

"You got it!" "Sure!" "Glad to have you home, Dad!" "Oh gee, is that the time?"

Before Kat could blink, they vanished in a chorus of slamming doors.

Lynch chuckled quietly. He put down his bag near the door and hung up his coat. Then, without a word, he walked to the sofa. He picked up the remote control, and turned off the video that was still playing, long forgotten.

Kat squirmed uncomfortably as she waited.

Finally, Lynch crossed over to her.

"I understand, Kat," he said, breaking the silence with a sigh. "Truly, I do. Can you imagine how many times I've had the same thoughts myself over the years? A normal job, a house in the suburbs, a couple of kids?

"But that's not for people like us. We've got a different path to follow. Different responsibilities. We're the ones who keep those people safe so they can have those lives . . . and stay alive to enjoy them."

Lynch paused. As usual, his face gave little indication of the thoughts running through his mind.

"Where would you kids be today if I had chosen that route years ago?" he continued. "Where will countless other people be if you try to choose it now?"

No sooner had Lynch finished than the words poured out of Kat in a rush. "I hear what you're saying, Mister

Lynch—really," she said. "But with all due respect, that's a load of bull!"

Lynch reacted with surprise. He wasn't used to hearing even such mild euphemisms from Kat.

"First of all," Kat said, "you and I are *not* the same. I'm not about to go spend my life as some sort of government super-spy. I want to help people, sure. But you're not going to find me running some ultra-top-secret unit at I.O. for years and years. I respect you—a lot—and we share some of the same values, but there's no way that we're the same person or that we're going to make the same decisions.

"Second of all, like I told the team, I have no intention of leaving. Taking a job is not the same as busting up Gen[13]. I'll be here when you need me. But it can't be *all* that I do."

Lynch shook his head impatiently. "Kat, you have to be practical. If you think this through . . ."

"I *have* thought it through!" she answered. "I mean, think back to when we moved to New York. Weren't you the one who said that, now that we didn't have to run anymore, you wanted us out there living our lives?

"Well, that's what I'm doing. I'm living my life. And you know what? In its own way, it's scarier than facing a *hundred* I.O.'s!"

Kat's voice trailed off. She stared down at her feet, and her words grew more quiet. "That's why I need you to understand. See, even if you don't agree. . . . Even if you can't be happy for me . . .

". . . I could really use your support right now . . ."

Lynch frowned. He thought long and hard.

"Your mind is made up, isn't it?" he said.

"Yes."

"There's nothing I can say to change it."

"No."

"All right then," he said. "I still think it's a bad idea. However, if it's that important to you, then go do what you have to do."

Kat rushed forward and threw her arms around her surprised mentor. "Thank you!" she yelled, before releasing him and dashing off down the hall. "I've got to go write a resume!"

Off in her bedroom, Roxy took her ear away from the door. She lifted her hand and, with a sniffle, wiped away a tear.

CHAPTER 4

T he fleet ballistic missile submarine USS *Kolodny* was not a small ship. The *Kolodny* was three stories tall and, if you could stand it up on end, it would be taller than the Washington Monument. For the past two months, it had been home to about one hundred and sixty crewmen, who had spent almost all of that time underwater.

Apart from the crew, the sub was also home to a fully-functional nuclear reactor, which provided its power, as well as twenty-four Trident ballistic missiles. That translated into twenty-four nuclear ICBM missiles, every single one of which had an effective range of more than four thousand miles and the capacity to destroy a city.

Essentially, the mission of the *Kolodny* was to avoid human contact. In the time since the sub had left its home port in Groton, Connecticut, it had crisscrossed the North Atlantic, over and over, along a variety of routes. It wasn't that the ship was going somewhere in particular. The idea was for the submarine and its cargo to avoid being found.

Many of the crewmen stationed on the *Kolodny* had originally joined the Navy looking for adventure, only to discover that what they'd really signed up for was just a job. Countless months of routine maneuvers and tedious maintenance work had managed to reduce even the responsibility of manning a submarine that could wipe out a small country to nothing more than "same old, same old." Even though all of the crewmen wore dosimeters attached to their uniforms, to warn of any potential radiation leaks, it was really just a standard precaution. The shielding on the reactor and the missiles was strong enough that there was never any problem. The last time an American nuclear submarine had sunk was all the way back in 1968.

The *Kolodny* was cruising along at a comfortable speed of twenty knots, nine hundred feet below the surface of the ocean, when all of that changed.

Not that the problem was the fault of the captain or crew. For the past year and a half, the *Kolodny* had been under the command of Captain Robert Tyler. Tyler ran a tight, disciplined ship, with good morale and a model safety record. A beefy man in his late thirties, Tyler easily fit the mold of what, in an earlier time, would have been called a man whose mistress was the sea.

In some ways, actually, the description was almost too apt for his taste. Back in high school, Bob Tyler had been quite the golden boy, the captain of the school's football team (a captain even then!). And, to no one's surprise, his heart belonged to the head cheerleader, Chrissy Regan. Their relationship was more than a cliche, though, and it continued long after graduation, when Chrissy went off to college and Tyler joined the service. They continued to write and call each other regularly, and they saw each other as often as their personal commitments allowed.

When Tyler's tour of duty ended, though, the friction began. Chrissy had assumed that once Tyler's obligation to the Navy ended, he'd be coming home. He'd get a job, they'd get married, and they would settle down to raise children. However, Tyler had been bitten by the bug. He had his eye on an officer's track, and couldn't wait to re-up so that he could get back to sea. He hadn't imagined that it would interfere with any of their plans for their future. Lots of the guys were married, like Smitty or Dwight or Aryeh, and when they were at sea, their wives lived comfortably and waited for them in the homes that the Navy provided back in port. But Chrissy had other ideas. After so much time apart, she wanted a family that wouldn't be separated from each other for weeks or months at a time.

They tried to keep things going after that, but the lengthy absences and failure to compromise took their toll. Finally, Crissy gave Tyler an ultimatum: her or the sea.

The sea won.

Captain Tyler wasn't the first to man the bridge of the *Kolodny*, but it was his baby now—with all the pride, worry, and joy that implied. The Captain was in the mess hall, perusing the leftovers from that night's dinner, when things started to go bad. There was a fair selection of midnight rations (or "mid-rats," as they were known to the crew) to choose from. After a bit of consideration, Tyler stabbed a slice to meatloaf and added it to a late-night sandwich. As he squirted on some ketchhup as the finishing touch, he talked baseball with the ship's supply officer.

". . . Sorry, Captain. Looks like my Yanks are gonna go all the way again this year."

"I don't know, Evans. Don't all those pennants get monotonous, year after year? The nice thing about us Bostonians is that being Red Sox fans teaches us humility."

The two shared a laugh at that. But as the Captain looked back down at the table, he suddenly noticed the dampness on the floor. It was probably nothing—a simple spill, or leftover moisture from the last cleaning crew. But still . . .

The Captain called over the seaman who was manning the mess hall. The seaman didn't know how to explain it either.

That was when the alarms started to sound.

The Captain dropped his sandwich and ran to the bridge. His feet splashed through water all the way along. It was almost ankle-deep in some places.

The sub had become a flurry of action. Everyone aboard was moving. Running. Scrambling. Sealing hatches. Manning controls. Trying to do whatever they could, without really knowing what was going on.

The bridge was even worse. Everyone was talking at once, trying to figure out what was happening while trying simultaneously to correct it.

Even as he stepped onto the bridge, the Captain took command of the situation. "Status report?"

"We're taking on water, sir," said the executive officer.

"I can see that, Roman. Tell me something I don't know." The Captain turned to the planesman. "Initiate emergency procedures. Blow the tanks." Blowing the tanks—forcing high-pressure air into the ballast tanks—would displace the sea water that they currently held and make the sub more buoyant. It was the fastest way to bring the ship to the surface.

"We already did, sir," the planesman replied, trying to keep himself under control. "It's not working. This isn't a minor leak. We're taking on water at least as fast as we're pumping it out of the tanks."

"Have we isolated the breach?"

"Breach*es*, sir," said the chief engineer. He listened to his headset for a moment. "At least two. One in the engine room, lower level. The other on the upper deck."

"Two? Where the hell did they come from?"

"I don't know."

"How big?"

"One's about three feet long and a foot wide. The other one's bigger."

"My God . . ."

The Captain placed his hands on one of the consoles. He bent down and hung his head as the full enormity of the situation hit him with the force of a sledgehammer. But he also remembered that he didn't have the luxury of being able to indulge his own feelings. He had a duty to uphold.

Captain Tyler stood erect, his jaw set. "Radioman?"

"Mayday signal already sent, sir. Continuing to send at one-minute intervals."

"Good. Roman, order the men into evacuation gear. I

want all non-essential personnel lined up in an orderly fashion at the escape trunks. It's going to take time to pressurize and de-pressurize the airlocks for each group. So let's get them started now."

"Aye aye, sir. But you know we're at nine hundred feet. Even if they get out, the pressure out there—"

"I know. But right now, we don't have a choice. Meanwhile, planesman, throttleman—"

"Sir."

"Angle us up toward the surface. Throttle on full. Let's try to get up there the hard way."

"Sir, we've got electrical failures starting to hit all over the place. At the rate we're taking on water, we can't possibly make it . . ."

"No, but maybe we can get high enough to give us better odds for evacuation."

"Aye aye, sir."

The Captain said a silent prayer.

The evacuation started out in every bit as orderly a fashion as the Captain had demanded. The *Kolodny* was manned by a carefully-screened, highly disciplined crew. Standard Naval emergency procedures had been laid out in detail and practiced in countless training sessions, until they were second nature. Those procedures were critical now.

Yet, as the water rose down below, the orderly evacuation dissolved into chaos. Fights broke out among the crew, as the desperate men tore at each other to be the next ones through the escape hatches. Panic turned people who had been friends only hours before into animals battling for survival.

In all the commotion, no one noticed three twelve-year-olds, two girls and one boy, standing in the shadows. The trio watched the scene with impassive expressions.

It took three hours for rescue craft to reach the USS *Kolodny's* last known position. Out of the crew of one hundred and sixty, they found seventeen survivors.

Captain Robert Tyler was not among them.

It would take several hours more before deep-sea recovery equipment could be deployed to locate the wreck of the *Kolodny* on the ocean floor. Robot probes explored the ins and outs of the lost submarine, sending video images to the surface, where the recovery crew could puzzle over the tragedy and try to uncover some clue as to what had happened.

But as the robots made their way through the *Kolodny*, their most chilling discovery wasn't any new revelation about what caused the submarine to sink.

It was the fact that, of the twenty-four nuclear missiles that the *Kolodny* had carried . . .

. . . only twenty-three were still on board.

". . . calling this the worst American Naval tragedy in more than thirty years. Government sources are declining to release the names of those who were lost at this time, waiting until they can first contact the victims' families. However, we have confirmation that the death toll has already climbed to well over one hundred, and recovery efforts are still underway.

"Investigators are still trying to determine the cause of the deadly accident. This was the scene at dawn, when combined rescue teams from . . ."

Lynch sat on the sofa and slowly took a sip from his cup of black coffee. He watched the early morning newscast through narrowed eyes, digesting the information.

Lynch didn't know about the missing Trident missile. It wasn't the sort of tidbit that was being handed over to the media, so the newscast made no mention of it. Still, the information that was reported was more than enough to capture Lynch's attention anyway.

Several feet away, Sarah stretched and twisted her body before the picture window that looked out over the concrete canyons of Manhattan. Her routine wasn't quite t'ai-chi, and it wasn't quite yoga, although it incorporated aspects of both. Sarah preferred to do this part of her exercise routine here, rather than in the room that housed their gym equipment, to take advantage of the more attractive view that the picture window afforded. Which was ironic, actually, since Sarah generally worked her way through her routine with her eyes closed, seemingly oblivious to everything around her.

It was a familiar scene, one that could be found in the apartment almost every day at about this time. Ordinarily, unless you counted Grunge's snoring (which had been known to elicit complaints from people two blocks away), the rest of the apartment was quiet in the early hours. Most members of Gen[13] weren't exactly morning people.

If truth be told, Sarah treasured this time of day. No one would describe her as shy or retiring, especially when something threatened one of her causes or principles. Yet, compared to people like Grunge or Roxy, she was positively stoic. The quiet time gave Sarah the opportunity to center herself and set the tone for the day. It was a big part of what made her seem so much older than her teenage years. *That, and boundless wisdom and maturity*, she told herself with a smile.

In a couple of hours, the apartment would erupt into a raucous din of noise, music, and conversation. This time, on the other hand, was for her.

Or maybe not just for her. Sarah was also glad for the daily time with Lynch, who routinely rose even before she did. Lynch was a man of even fewer words than Sarah, and a hard man to know. They never said much of anything to each other during this time, other than wishing each other a good morning. But the simple proximity as they went through their morning routines with no one else around had given them something in common, and built some sort of a bond between them.

Today was different, though. The peace was shattered as Kat came barrelling out of her room like a runaway freight train.

"It's after eight! Why didn't anyone wake me? I've gotta go! I'm going to be late! Where's my left shoe?"

Kat was dressed to the nines for her day of interviews—or mostly dressed, anyway. She was still buttoning up her white, ruffled blouse as she simultaneously dashed around the apartment, gathering her things. She started to apply lipstick while she ran toward the kitchen.

Sarah continued to do her lazy stretches without opening her eyes. Lynch spent another minute or so watching the newscast, until the story changed to a feature on high-priced holiday fashions for dogs. He used the remote to switch off the television, then took another sip of his coffee.

Kat came tearing back into the room, stuffing a bagel into her mouth with one hand while she pinned a stack of resumes under the opposite arm. She juggled it all successfully as she snatched her suit jacket off the end of the sofa. But when she raised her arms to put the jacket on, she lost her grip on the stack of resumes. They drifted down like Autumn leaves to scatter on the floor.

"No!" she shrieked through a mouthful of bagel.

Kat fell to her knees and frantically started to gather up the fallen paper. She was about halfway through when Lynch said, "You can't go."

Kat froze for a moment, then went back to picking up resumes. "Oh, come on, Mister Lynch," she mumbled through the bagel. "We went through all of this last night!"

"Yes, but that was last night. Things have changed."

"Changed? What kind of things could have changed?"

"A nuclear submarine sank in the North Atlantic this morning."

"Wow, that's terrible. Anyone hurt?"

"Over one hundred dead."

"Wow." She started tapping on the sides of the pile of paper to straighten out the stack. "And . . . ?"

" 'And' what?"

" 'And' . . . why would it affect my job interviews?"

Lynch looked surprised. "Kat, nuclear submarines

don't just sink. They have multiple redundant back-up systems. I think it bears looking into."

Kat thought for a moment, her head cocked to the side. "Isn't the Navy doing that?"

"Well, yes, but . . ."

Kat slipped the resumes into a shoulder bag. "Was there some kind of giant, radioactive dinosaur involved?"

"What?!"

"Then why does the Navy need us getting in their way? It's not like anyone's in any immediate danger. I'm really sorry it happened, but unfortunately, the damage is already done. There's nothing we can do about it. Aha!" Kat pointed triumphantly at her missing shoe. She reached under a bar stool with her foot and wriggled her way into it. "All that's left now is figuring out what happened. I'm sure the Navy's got people who are a lot better qualified than I am to do that."

"Perhaps, but they certainly don't have anyone better qualified to deal with the people behind it."

"If there *are* people behind it. You're assuming someone set this up. But how can you tell? For all we know, this could just be an accident. Like with that Russian sub that sank a while back."

Lynch's face tightened. "You're missing the point, Kat. Something's in the wind. To have you potentially inaccessible when it hits, well, it's just not a good idea."

Kat opened the closet and grabbed her coat. "You didn't think it was a good idea before the submarine sank either. Forgive me for asking, but are you sure that isn't influencing your interpretation of the whole submarine thing? Maybe just a little bit?"

Lynch inhaled sharply. "I've been doing this a long time, Caitlin. Longer than you've been alive. I'd like to think I'm a little more professional than that."

Even in her hurry, the yawning pit in her stomach told Kat that she'd gone too far. She stopped cold, right in the middle of slipping her arm into the sleeve of her coat.

"You're right," she said, even though she didn't really believe it completely. "I'm sorry."

The two stared at each other for a moment.

"Look, how about a compromise?" Kat offered. She shrugged the coat onto her shoulders, then pulled a pen and one of the resumes out of her bag. She stepped quickly over to the bar, laid the resume face down, and started writing on the back. "Until we know for sure that anything's going on, there isn't much for us to do anyway, right?

"So, here—I'll write down my schedule and all the places where I'll be. That way, if anything does break, you can track me down, and I'll come straight home. I promise. But meanwhile, during the time that I'd just be sitting around waiting anyhow, I can go ahead and make it to my interviews. Okay?"

Lynch didn't say anything. Kat decided to take the lack of protest as grudging agreement.

She finished writing, and gave the paper a quick pat before heading for the door. "There!" she said. "Now, I really do need to run. Wish me luck, guys!" She gave them a quick wave. Then, she was gone, the door slamming closed behind her. Of course, in her haste, Kat's super-strong slam made the entire wall shake and broke the lock again. But that wasn't really at the top of anyone's mind right now.

Lynch stood there, just watching the door. After a moment, he turned and stormed off into the other room.

Finally alone, Sarah opened her eyes, and picked up the small towel that lay at her feet. Neither Kat nor Lynch had sought to bring her into the argument, and that suited her just fine. She used the towel to wipe down her face and neck, draped it over her shoulders, and stretched out to melt into the comfortable sofa.

Once she was settled in, Sarah reached down to the floor and picked up one of the dozens of pornographic magazines that Bobby had strewn around the apartment as "surprises" to tempt Grunge when he woke up. She flipped idly through pages upon pages of naked women who were bending themselves at awkward angles across motorcycles and pool tables.

At another time, Sarah would probably be mortally offended at this exploitation of women. But in the quiet, and with her body feeling so relaxed, she just couldn't muster up the energy. Instead, as she scanned the pictures, Sarah contented herself with noting the fact that she just didn't get it. Oh, the women were attractive enough, and Sarah shared the guys' interest in such things. But there was no . . . subtlety here, no romance. Were men really that obvious?

She thought of Grunge. *I guess that answers that,* she thought with a smile.

Since the photos didn't hold her interest, Sarah decided to amuse herself by reading the captions instead:

"*A devotée of classical music, we asked Bambi whether she saw* Amadeus. *'Anthony Schaeffer is a jerk!' says the tawny eighteen-year-old. 'Mozart wasn't some cheap vulgarian. He was one of the greatest musical geniuses of the ages!' "*

The caption accompanied a photo of the "tawny eighteen-year-old devotée of classical music" spread-eagled across a baby grand piano, her hair cascading across the keys.

Lynch came storming back into the room, carrying his coat and looking determined. Without so much as a pause, he headed straight for the front door. "I'm going out," he said without looking at Sarah. "There are some things I need to check into."

"Whatever," Sarah replied, in an off-handed tone. To her way of thinking, the morning's events all made for entirely too much angst before breakfast.

Once the door slammed behind Lynch, Sarah closed the magazine and let it drop to the floor. She peeled herself off the sofa with a languid air and a knowing smile.

"You're just in a mood because you know she's right,"

Sarah said to the space her absent mentor left behind. "Otherwise, you never would've let her leave."

Sarah headed for the gym. She still had a workout to finish.

CHAPTER 5

At precisely five minutes past nine, J. B. Heffler looked at his vague reflection in the frosted glass of his office door, and ran a hand through his thick, gray hair. Ever since "the MBAs took over" (as he put it) back in the 1980s, his work day had started at nine o'clock sharp. So he made it a point to arrive exactly five minutes late each day.

Once his hair was arranged the way he liked it, J. B. pulled the keys from his pocket and unlocked his office door. J. B. smiled as he inhaled the musty odor from his cluttered office, then stepped inside and closed the door. He took off his heavy winter coat and held it in one hand while he took down a hanger from the hook on the back of the door. He was just draping the coat over the hanger when he jumped at the sound of a voice behind him.

"Good morning, J. B."

J. B. turned to see Lynch leaning comfortably against a file cabinet. "Oh, it's you, Jack," he said with a playful smile. "You need to watch that. I'm not a young man, you know."

Lynch returned the smile, although his eyes still showed the seriousness of his purpose. "Now, now. You've still got a couple of good years left in you, at least."

In many ways, J. B. was a relic from another time, when newspapers relied on paper rather than electronic files. J. B. had run the morgue at the *New York News* for as long as anyone could remember, maintaining, updating, and indexing the archives of every single story the paper had ever run.

As computers came to play increasingly large roles in newspaper production, it seemed as though the need for a morgue—or an archivist—would have faded into oblivion, right alongside linotype presses and teletype machines. Electronic filing of stories meant that every story from the day's newspaper could be added to archival databases as soon as the editors approved them for publication. The days of clipping and filing columns of newsprint were long gone.

However, while the technology might have changed, the need for someone who could organize vast quantities of information and find it at a moment's notice hadn't gone away. If anything, in the midst of the "information revolution," the need had grown exponentially greater. J. B. had stayed on top of the new technologies as each had been introduced, adapting to each new direction as it came along and disregarding the ones that soon disappeared.

If that weren't enough to guarantee J. B.'s job security, there was also the fact that the electronic archive only went back eleven years. Most of the material from the newspaper's 175-year history was still available only on microfilm or yellowing scraps of paper. J. B. had been given managerial responsibility for digitizing the entire archive, a project that, conservatively, was estimated to take until at least 2022, long after he was scheduled to retire. Not that anyone could imagine him ever retiring. It was far more likely that when the time came, he would pass away and be quietly filed under "H."

For, you see, J. B. was a self-confessed information junkie of the highest order. His head held a bewildering array of trivia that he could produce off the tip of his tongue without even having to think hard. Whether the topic was obscure quotes from past Middle East leaders or the winners of every Kentucky Derby of the twentieth century (win, place, and show, including their respective running times), J. B. was the man to call. And if there was a question on any topic that he couldn't answer off the top of his head, he invariably knew where to look.

Still, the fact remained that, with technology making access to past material increasingly easy, J. B. was one of a dying breed. When Lynch stopped to think about that point, it saddened him. Part of the reason stemmed from the fact that, after more than twenty years of occasional contacts, he'd grown to genuinely like the old man. On a more practical level, though, J. B. was one of Lynch's most valuable resources for information, particularly when he didn't want to go through more official governmental channels. Mystery novels so often made a big deal about alliances between intrepid detectives and crusading reporters, but the truth was that Lynch found reporters to be a pain.

Especially the crusading ones.

The main problem with reporters was that they were always looking for a story—that next big scoop. Sure, they had access to a broad variety of sources. But for every answer a reporter had ever provided to Lynch, it had always come along with ten or twenty additional questions. Considering how much of Lynch's time was spent in covert operations, those were questions that he had no desire to answer.

Archivists like J. B. were a different story. Where reporters were interested in scoops, archivists were interested in information and history. Plus, there was the fact that people who were nosy and talkative tended not to gravitate toward the quiet, solitary kinds of work to be found in newspaper morgues. In all the time that Lynch had known J. B., he'd never once asked a question that Lynch didn't feel at liberty to answer.

When J. B. did eventually decide to pack it all in, Lynch would miss him.

"So, what brings you to my little hovel this time, Jack?" asked J. B.

"What always brings me here, J. B.? Information."

"Giving or getting?"

Lynch reached down to produce two well-aged bottles of Glenfiddich.

"Ah, well. Same as always," said J. B. "Always getting, never giving. But always I tell you, Jack: You don't need to bribe me anymore."

"It's not a bribe. It's fair payment for a valuable service."

"Ah. Well, in that case . . ." J. B. took the two bottles and stashed them in the bottom drawer of his file cabinet. Once they were securely stored away, J. B. walked around his desk, turning on the computer along the way. He sat down in his chair, and watched the machine warm up. "What are you looking for today?"

"A submarine sank early this morning. The USS *Kolodny.*"

"Hmm. This morning, eh? Let's see if a story's been filed yet." J. B.'s fingers ran over the keyboard, and an index of the day's news stories appeared on the screen. "Yup, slated for page one of the afternoon edition. Looks like we already got a first draft from the reporter—oh, Michael Simons, he's pretty good—and a revised version with a first pass of editor's notes."

"Can you pull them both up for me?"

"Sure."

With a couple of clicks, J. B. opened two windows of text on the screen. He got up from his chair to let Lynch sit in front of the screen. J. B. took a hefty reference book down from the top of one of the file cabinets. He busied himself with digging up some statistics that had been requested the night before, and basically proceeded to mind his own business.

Lynch began by studying the revised version of the story. It included a few quotes from members of the recovery team, but other than that, presented essentially the same information as had been in the television report.

Next he compared the revised version and the original,

side by side. Sometimes, the first draft included facts that were absent from subsequent versions. When that happened, it was generally for one of two reasons. One possibility was that the text had been cut to fit the available space on the page. The second was because someone didn't like something that had been said, and the offending bits were cut because of either inside influence or fear of a lawsuit.

In this case, however, the differences between the two versions were minor. A few typographical and grammatical errors had been fixed, but other than that, they were largely identical. Apparently, J. B. wasn't the only one at the paper who thought that Michael Simons was a pretty good reporter.

The public sources were starting to make it look as though Kat was right about the submarine. No one was talking about it as anything more than an accident. Still, Lynch couldn't shake the feeling that something more was going on.

Lynch frowned. Could the sinking of the submarine have been nothing more than a freak, one-in-a-million malfunction? Was Kat correct? And if so, could it be that Kat was right about Lynch's own motivations, too? Was this all really about nothing more than cutting the apron strings and letting the young woman leave the nest?

Lynch didn't buy it. But at the same time, he had to admit that he couldn't be sure. He needed to dig deeper to find the truth. And that meant drawing on sources that even the *New York News* couldn't access.

Lynch reached into his pocket and took out a cell phone. To all appearances, the device was the same sort of telephone that millions of other people carried around each day, frequently annoying everyone around them in the process. Actually, though, the insides of the phone consisted of a scaled-down version of the military TAC-SAT technology that allowed field operatives to be in immediate telephone contact with their home bases from anywhere in the world via tactical satellite. Lynch's phone didn't have the reach of true TAC-SAT equipment, and the protection against eavesdroppers wasn't quite as secure; the full-blown version would have required a satellite dish and mobile power source, all of which would have defeated the purpose of a discreet, portable communication device. But its built-in encryption software and random routing through satellite connections were usually more than enough to serve his needs. Together, they provided him with easy access to a secure, essentially untraceable phone line no matter where he might be.

Lynch punched in a telephone number from memory. It was a number that he hadn't used in a long time. However, long ago, he'd learned the value of keeping all of his important contact numbers in his head, rather than committing them to paper or an electronic address book.

He listened to the phone ring twice before someone picked up on the other end. "Greenberg," said the voice. It wasn't easy to make a two-syllable name sound harried, but the person on the phone had done it.

"Kal, it's Lynch."

"Aw, geez, Lynch. I can't talk to you now. Do you know what kind of hell is breaking loose over here?"

"No, Kal, I don't. That's why I thought I'd cut through the bureaucratic nonsense and call someone in Naval Intel who might give me some straight answers."

"Oh, for . . . It might surprise you to learn that there's a reason they call it 'Naval *Intelligence*.' You think I can just hand out classified information over the phone to anyone who asks for it?"

"I'm not just anyone."

"No, I know you're not just anyone."

"Let's remember who tipped you off when the Walkers were selling your secrets to the Russians."

"Yeah, I kn—"

"It would be a shame if our lines of communication had to shut down."

Greenberg didn't say anything. Only the hubbub of

background noise indicated that the call hadn't been cut off.

Finally, Greenberg spoke. "This is a secure line?"

"That's why I called your cell instead of your office line. There won't even be a record of the call in the daily logs."

"All right. Call me back in two minutes."

Lynch's lips formed a tight smile as he pressed the button to disconnect the call. He put down the phone and turned to J. B. "J. B., I hate to ask, but would you mind going to get yourself a cup of coffee for a few minutes?"

J. B. laid down the papers he'd been reviewing. "That's right," he muttered good-naturedly. "Take over an old man's desk. Kick him out of his own office. This is what they teach you when you get to be a big-shot spy?" With a wink, J. B. left the office and closed the door behind him.

Despite himself, Lynch had to chuckle. He looked back at the computer screen and glanced through the index of the stories that had been filed so far for today's newspaper. He wanted to see if there had been any other unexplained occurrences that could be tied to the incident with the submarine.

So far, though, there was little that looked promising. There were the weekly features like the crossword puzzle and articles on gardening that had been written far in advance. The hard news that had already been filed consisted of the usual sorts of budget wrangling between the President and Congress, a piece on rising crime rates, strife in the Middle East, and that sort of thing. Nothing terribly remarkable, other than the *Kolodny* disaster.

He pulled up the indexes from the previous several days. He leaned back in the chair and started to scan through them as he hit the "redial" button on his phone.

This time, the phone on the other end picked up on the first ring. "Greenberg."

"Lynch."

"What do you want to know?"

"The *Kolodny*."

"You and everyone else in the world. It's a madhouse around here. We've got D.O.D. breathing down our necks, the White House calling every ten minutes . . . Maybe we could dig up some answers for them if we didn't have to spend all our time answering the phone."

"That's a lot of fuss for an accident."

Greenberg snorted. "Yeah, right."

"You're not convinced."

"To tell you the truth, I'm not sure what the hell it is. But it's sure no accident."

"Bomb?"

"Not like any I've ever seen. No blast radius, none of the scorching or scoring that you'd get with a bomb."

"So what, then?"

"Damned if I know. Two breaches in the hull. Big ones. One of them measured out at point-nine meters long, the other at two-point-six."

"Mm. But not a bomb."

"Nah. Preliminary investigation of the scene shows multiple stress points at the seams between the plates, loosened rivets . . . It's like the damned thing just shook itself apart."

"Maybe someone sabotaged it before it left port. Weakened the seams, loosened the rivets."

"The *Kolodny* left port sixty-three days ago. Even if it took this long for the undersea pressure to take its toll— which isn't bloody likely—there's regular maintenance that happens every day on those subs. There's no way that kind of damage would have gone undetected this long. Whatever happened, happened last night."

"And that's why you're so sure this wasn't an accident."

"Well, that and one other thing."

"What's that?"

"The part we're not giving to the press."

"Which is . . . ?"

"There's a Trident II missile unaccounted for."

Lynch gave a low whistle. "So that's why all the pressure from the Brass."

"You got it. They get a mite touchy when we can't find one of their nukes."

"Do you realize what you're saying?"

"No, Lynch, I don't realize what I'm saying. Tell me what I'm saying," Greenberg said, exasperated. "Of course I know what I'm saying. Those holes in the sub aren't big enough for a Trident to just fall out. Someone took it. That means there's a rogue warhead out there. We don't know who's got it, we don't know how they did it, we don't know who they're going to shoot it at, and it's got our signature on it."

"Besides that," Lynch replied. "From the way you were describing things, I assumed this was a suicide mission. Someone infiltrated the crew, did the damage, and probably died with the rest of them. But that's not it.

"If that missile is gone, then whoever took it survived to get off. And they managed to take a 130,000-pound missile off a sub from one thousand feet down."

"That's about the size of it," Greenberg agreed. "Not exactly a modus opperandi I'm familiar with. Know any roving packs of terrorist killer whales?"

"Anyone take responsibility yet?"

"The usuals. 'Retribution against the imperialist American government, yadda, yadda, yadda.' But they're all blowing smoke. None of them knew about the Trident."

"So what now?"

"What do you think? Publicly, we chalk the whole thing up to a 'tragic malfunction,' honor the heroic dead, and swear to make sure the equipment is upgraded so that it never happens again. Privately, we work our butts off to find out who did this and take our damned nuke back."

"Hmmmm," said Lynch. "There's still one thing that bothers me."

"Just one?"

"This doesn't add up as an isolated incident. Have there been any other . . . unusual events lately?"

Greenberg laughed without mirth. "If 'unusual events' like this were going on before, I'd have quit by now. Nah, it's been downright dull around here."

"Well, let me know if there's anything I can do to help out with this thing."

"Gee, you could find the nuke," Greenberg said, with more than a trace of sarcasm in his voice. "That'd be good. Yeah, that would be a big help."

Lynch smiled. "I'll see what I can do. Thanks, Kal."

Greenberg hung up. A moment later, Lynch did the same.

Lynch sat in the chair with his fingertips pressed together, deep in thought. So, he had been right, after all. There *was* more going on than met the eye. Somehow, though, he didn't take much satisfaction in being right about this one. Given the way that the stakes were rapidly mounting, he would just as soon have been wrong.

It wasn't just that, though. He still believed what he said to Greenberg. It didn't make sense for this to be just one isolated incident. With something so big brewing, there had to be other pieces falling into place, other traces to be found.

Lynch looked back at the computer screen. He'd scanned yesterday's news index while talking to Greenberg, but nothing exceptional stood out there either.

Lynch clicked back to the day before. And there it was, splashed across the front page:

MURDER ON CAPITOL HILL!
Sturmer Dead
Police Seek Mystery Slayer

Washington was rocked this morning by the brazen murder of Representative Charlene Sturmer (D-Colo.). Not only was reaction provoked by the death of the popular Congresswoman, but also by the location where the crime took place: the halls of the Capitol building itself . . .

Lynch stared at the account, his jaw hanging open. How could he have not jumped at this story before?

Then he remembered. Two days ago, he'd been boarding an airplane under an assumed name, for a twenty-hour flight back to the United States. He'd never seen the news that day. Since then, the follow-up stories had just made reference to Sturmer's murder without giving details. He'd assumed it was a more run-of-the-mill crime, albeit with a famous victim. Sturmer wasn't the first famous person to be murdered, and she probably wouldn't be the last.

Lynch cursed himself for not checking into the details sooner. The crime bore all the signs of being committed by a super-powered being—possibly a gen-active like Gen[13] and himself—and the incident on the *Kolodny* did, too.

How many others have I missed? he thought.

Lynch was devouring every word of the article on Sturmer's death when J. B. walked in. "Knock knock," J. B. said. "Okay to come back now?"

Lynch replied without looking up. "How do I perform a general search through the archive?"

J. B. stepped around the desk and placed his hands on the keyboard. "What are you looking for?"

"Politicians who've died in the past six months."

By the time they finished the search, Lynch had what he was looking for. Four Senators and Representatives had died within the past six months. The deaths happened in various parts of the country, and were spread over time. Five months ago, Representative Evan Lowenthal of Missouri died in a car accident on a dark country road. Four months ago, Senator Hilton Wong of California died from complications stemming from a stroke. Two months ago, Senator Martin Cheswick of New York committed suicide, a tragedy that was being blamed on a secret addiction to pain killers; apparently, he'd developed a dependence on them after a recent bout of surgery. Finally, two days ago, there was Charlene Sturmer's murder at the Capitol.

The different settings and causes, coupled with the time lags between the deaths, meant that no one had spent much time trying to connect them before. Not to mention the fact that it was only four people. However, when Lynch and J. B. compared the Congressional death rate to other six-month periods, they found that four deaths was at least twice as many as had occurred during any comparable period in the last ten years.

"Of course, with numbers this small, 'twice as many' only means two more than usual," J. B. reminded Lynch.

Still, Lynch felt he was onto something. Three of the four victims also shared something in common: They all sat on budget allocation committees.

"Sure, but that's only three out of four," J. B. said. "What about the other one?"

"Wong was eighty-four years old," Lynch replied.

"So you think that one really was natural causes?"

"A stroke at eighty-four? It's certainly possible. If so, someone could have taken advantage of it to break the pattern and throw off suspicion."

J. B. rubbed the back of his neck. "I don't know, Jack. Everything you're saying is possible, I suppose. But what you're basing it on, well, calling it slim would be a compliment. You might be able to get the conspiracy nuts in your corner, but you'd have a hard time convincing anyone else."

"You're right," Lynch admitted. "That's why I'm going to gather more evidence."

"What do you mean?"

Lynch rose from the chair and walked to the door. "Cheswick died here in New York.

"I'm going to examine the scene."

CHAPTER 6

Bobby was sitting on the sofa with his feet up, an un-plugged electric guitar on his lap. He accompanied himself quietly as his soft voice carried the lyrics and melody to a song of his own creation:

> *"Been down*
> *This road so many times before*
> *I've found*
> *Don't wanna be here anymore*
> *This world*
> *Is filled with dross dressed up as gold*
> *This girl*
> *Could mean salvation from the cold*
>
> *"So hold me*
> *And tell me*
> *Can you understand*
> *The little boy*
> *Behind the face*
> *Of the angry young man . . ."*

Abruptly, Bobby stopped playing. He left the guitar sitting on his lap as he reached over to pick up the pencil and yellow legal pad that lay on the sofa beside him. Chewing thoughtfully on the pencil's eraser, he studied the crossed-out lines and the scribbles upon scribbles that filled the top sheet of the pad.

Needs work, he thought.

VERSION 2.0

There were days when Bobby still allowed himself to dream rock star dreams. Sometimes, in his fantasies, he would play to packed arenas of fans who would sing along with every memorized word. At other times, he would imagine himself playing clubs small enough to watch the faces of the crowd as they gave themselves over to his music. But Bobby was also realistic enough to recognize the idle fantasies for what they were: pleasant daydreams to pass the time, rather than concrete action plans for the future.

To tell the truth, after years of practice, Bobby had actually gotten pretty good on the guitar. He didn't kid himself, though. He might be good enough to play for friends or his own amusement, but he knew he was no Dave Navarro or Jon Spencer. Not to mention the fact that his lyrics weren't nearly as strong as his playing.

"Dross?" he thought, scanning over the page of verse. He scrunched up his face in distaste and crossed out the offending line. *When have I ever used a word like "dross?"*

Bobby was pondering a replacement when Roxy slowly made her way into the room, yawning and stretching. She was still wearing the oversized pink t-shirt with the big picture of a puppy that she'd used as a nightshirt the night before. "Yo," she said in mid-yawn.

"Hey."

Roxy scratched her hair roughly to clear her head. She looked around through tossled hair and bleary eyes. "So where is everybody?"

"Sarah's in the kitchen. Grunge got up a little while ago, but then he looked around, screamed, and booked back into his room."

"Huh? What's up with that?"

"No idea," Bobby said with an innocent smile. He adjusted his feet on the two-foot-tall stack of porn magazines that he'd since collected from their strategically-placed positions around the room.

Roxy shrugged and stifled another yawn. "What about

81

Kat and Mister L? No way I'm up before them."

"Dream on. Sarah says my Dad's out investigating something or other. No telling when he'll get back. You know how he gets."

"And Kat?"

"She's got her job interviews today, rememeber?"

The reminder was like a jolt of caffeine through Roxy's system. She was suddenly alert, her eyes open wide. "She . . . went?"

"Yeah, sure. She had to get an early start." He used the neck of the guitar to gesture toward the bar. "Check it out—there's a list of her interviews over there. Looks like a pretty full day."

Roxy walked over to the bar and picked up the list. " 'Digiworld?' " she read. " 'Mousetrap?' "

"Computer companies, sounds like. Maybe she'll get lucky."

Roxy stared at the paper. "Yeah. Lucky . . . ," she muttered quietly.

"Hi, Rox," said Sarah, walking in from the other room. "There are still some pancakes left over, if you want to warm them up. Blueberry, your favorite."

"Thanks," Roxy said absently. "Maybe later. I, uh . . . I forgot something I gotta do in my room."

She looked away from her friends and hurriedly left the room.

Bobby and Sarah gave each other a curious glance.

"Am I crazy," Bobby asked, "or is everbody acting kind of weird today?"

"Everyone's acting kind of weird today," Sarah agreed. Then, she smirked and added, "But that doesn't mean you're not crazy."

Lynch paid the cab driver and stepped out onto the sidewalk. He looked up at the Wall Street office building, and weighed it over in his mind. The towering edifice didn't look like the sort of place where you'd be likely to find an after-school program. But then again, most people probably wouldn't have realized that there was a day care center in the Federal Building in Oklahoma City. That is, until some lunatic militiamen blew it up.

Lynch entered the lobby and walked past the guard station with a nod. He'd learned long ago that simply acting as though you knew where you were going was enough to avoid a lot of unwanted questions. He spotted the elevators out of the corner of his eye and walked purposefully into the nearest open car. Once inside, he pushed the button marked "17" and leaned back against the wall as the elevator rose.

The newspaper article had said that Cheswick fell from the seventeenth floor, but it hadn't mentioned the room number for the center he'd been visiting. Lynch didn't want to invite the guard's attention by checking the building directory in the lobby. After all, he was hoping that the after-school center would be closed in the morning, during school hours. That way, he could let himself in and have the chance to look around undisturbed. As a rule, it was usually best not to give security guards advance warning of intended breaking and entering.

Besides, he figured the room would be easy enough to find.

On the latter point, at least, he was wrong.

Lynch walked the halls of the seventeenth floor twice, but none of the signs on the doors sounded anything like an after-school program designed to keep children off drugs. There were a couple of unmarked doors, either of which could have been the right one. But there was no way to know which one it might be, or whether the program might be housed within the offices of one of the other companies on the floor.

Finally, Lynch put on his best attempt at a friendly smile, knocked on the door of an insurance company, and stepped inside.

The middle-aged receptionist put down a magazine and looked at him as though he'd just interrupted delicate surgery. "Yes?" she said, grudgingly. "Can I help you?"

"I'm sorry to bother you, but yes, I hope you can," Lynch said, keeping his smile in place. "I heard there's an after-school program around here somewhere . . . ? But I've been looking all over, and gosh, I can't seem to find it anywhere. Would you happen to know where it is?"

" 'After . . . ?' Oh, yeah. There was one for about a month or so, but it's long gone."

"Gone?"

"Yeah, right after that senator took a header out their window. Bad publicity, I guess."

" 'Header?' Oh! You mean Senator Cheswick? That business with Senator Cheswick happened here?"

"Yeah, right down that way." The receptionist pointed to her left.

"That way?" Lynch pointed in the same direction.

"Yeah. End of the hall down there."

"Oh, dear. How awful for all of you!"

The receptionist shrugged. "Politicians," she said.

"And the after-school program was only here for a month, you say?"

She shrugged again. "Who notices? Something like that, I guess."

"Well, then, I suppose it probably wouldn't have been right for my children anyway."

The corner of the receptionist's mouth twitched into something that vaguely resembled an indulgent smile.

"Well, thank you so much," Lynch said. "I'm so sorry to have taken up your time."

"No problem."

"Have a good day, now."

Lynch walked back out into the hall, letting the door swing closed behind him. He took a deep breath. He hated adopting that particular persona; it was just too alien to him, and too much work to keep up the sunny facade. But it did have its uses, and this time around, it got him the information he needed.

He walked briskly down to the end of the hall. There were two offices there, facing each other. The door to one office bore a brightly colored sign that proclaimed it the home of a graphics company. The other door was blank, and a quick try of the knob showed that it was locked tight.

Lynch knocked on the blank door, just in case anyone was inside. The last thing he wanted was to barge in on someone who'd want to know how Lynch got in without a key. He waited for an answer, and passed the time by looking casually around for passers-by or security cameras.

Once Lynch felt confident that no one was inside the office and no one was watching, he produced a set of lockpicks from his pocket. The door opened in no more time than it would have taken with a key. Lynch entered the office, and quietly closed and re-locked the door. No need to be interrupted without warning, after all.

Even a glance at the space was enough to confirm what the receptionist had told him. The room had been stripped bare, without a stick of furniture or forgotten knicknack to indicate that anyone had ever been here at all. Lynch suspected that the space had sat unused and untouched since the day the after-school program had cleared out. That might have been bad news for the landlord, but it was good news for Lynch, since it increased the chances that potential clues could still be waiting, undisturbed. The thought was enough to make Lynch thankful for the City's extravagantly high rents.

Doors from the main room led to two smaller rooms that made up the rest of the suite. Lynch stuck his head inside each of them in turn and looked around. One was a bathroom. The other was a small inner office. Each was as empty as the main room.

That alone was enough to intrigue Lynch further. Typically, when businesses vacate their space, they leave things behind, whether it's unneeded supplies or just stray scraps of packing materials. But this place had been cleaned out from top to bottom. Several hypothetical explanations ran through Lynch's mind. It was possible that the building simply had a very thorough cleaning staff, who had scoured the space after the center left. It was possible that whoever ran the program was compulsively neat. But the more interesting possibility was that the center was a front, and that the people behind it didn't want to leave any clues behind.

That would fit neatly with the receptionist's telling him that the center had only been here for about one month.

Lynch could imagine the political pressure that the New York Police Department had been under to close the Cheswick case quickly. With the national focus that the case had gained, the City government wasn't going to want to look inefficient in front of the State or the Feds. Given that, he could readily imagine that no one had looked too much further after the drug angle came to light. After all, a roomful of witnesses had seen Cheswick throw himself out the window of his own accord. The circumstances of Cheswick's death fit perfectly with a bad trip or a case of DT's. They probably never even got as far as checking into the background of the center itself.

But what if the center had been a fake? What if it had been set up for one purpose, and one purpose only:

To lure Senator Martin Cheswick to his death.

Once again, Lynch didn't have any hard evidence to back up any of his theories. It was all just conjecture at this point—conjecture that would be hard to prove. He suspected the name on the lease would prove to be phony, and he somehow doubted that whoever owned the center left a forwarding address. The empty office seemed to leave things at a dead end.

Still, it was only empty to the casual observer. No matter how hard the prior occupants might have tried to cover their tracks, it was likely that they had missed some tiny clues that could tell the tale. Finding those clues would mean combing every square inch of the office space in painstaking detail.

Lynch had the time.

•   •   •

Two hours later, Lynch had combed through a three-foot-wide swath of the tightly-knit carpet that stretched from one end of the main room to the other. He carried the fruits of his labor in a sealable plastic bag: three stray hairs that carried telltale DNA, some vaguely familiar metallic scrapings from the baseboard moulding that he couldn't quite identify, and a few other tiny clues that might yield something under further analysis.

That was one pass down. Three more, and he'd finish the room. Then he could go on to the others.

Lynch didn't mind the monotonous work. Years of intelligence work, sitting for hours in the back of disguised vans or piecing his way through mounds of data in search of the one golden needle in the haystack, had taught him the value of both patience and persistence. But the cramped muscles in Lynch's back also reminded him that he wasn't as young as he used to be.

He decided to stand up and stretch for a minute before getting back to the search. As he rose, his face passed by a heating vent, set in the wall about a foot above the floor. Something caught his eye.

Lynch kneeled back down to study the vent more closely. No, he hadn't imagined it. There was a funny shadow at the edge of one of the openings in the vent.

Lynch tried to reach the tiny object, but his fingers were too big to fit through the grating. He took out a pocket knife, opened the blade, and used it to probe inside the vent. It took several tries, but eventually, he succeeded in bringing the object far enough forward to grasp it with his fingertips. It was a slender black tube, less than an inch long and only a couple of milimeters in diameter. The front of the tube was open, covered by a tiny disc of glass or transparent plastic. The back was connected to a thin cable covered in black rubber insulation that led deeper into the vent.

Camera, Lynch thought. *With a fiber-optic cable.*

He tried giving the device a gentle tug, but there wasn't enough slack for the cable to extend more than a centimeter past the vent. In fact, it was only by keeping a tight grip, with his fingers pressed against the metal of the vent, that he could keep the cable extended at all. If he let go, it would have snapped back far enough into the vent that he wouldn't be able to reach it anymore.

This was no ordinary after-school program, he thought. *Is it still active?*

Are they still watching?

The best way to find answers, he figured, was to remove the cover of the vent and see what was inside. Without releasing his left hand's grip on the cable, Lynch used his right to close the blade of his pocket knife. That was easy enough. The next step was trickier, as he tried to open the knife's screwdriver blade with one hand. It slipped off his fingernail to snap shut twice. The third attempt seemed to be working better, though. The screwdriver had just barely managed to clear the body of the knife, when Lynch was startled by a voice.

A voice coming from inside the vent.

"Well, well. John Lynch," the electronically-disguised voice said with a sigh. "You know, I left this here in case anyone came snooping. But I never imagined it would be you."

It's a camera, all right, Lynch thought. *And a speaker.*

"Although I suppose I shouldn't be surprised. You never could keep your nose out of other people's business."

It's someone I know. Who—?

Lynch never got to finish the thought. Because that was the exact moment when a high-voltage charge surged through the vent. Every muscle of Lynch's body constricted in pain as the shock sent him flying.

Lynch landed hard on the floor.

He wasn't moving.

"Now, I suppose I'll have to deal with your brats, too, before they come looking for you," the voice continued.

There was another sigh.

"Life is just so complicated sometimes."

CHAPTER 7

"**Y**ou're hired," said the man in the suit.

"But . . . don't you want to see my resumé?"

"Oh, sure. You're hired."

Kat got up from her chair and picked up her bag.

"So, when would you like to start?" the man said. His voice had the vague, detached quality of someone speaking from far away in a daydream. "You could start now, if you want. We could get you set up now and you could get . . . y'know, started. When would be a good time for you to start?"

Kat gave him an icy stare. "Oh, I don't know," she said, with an edge in her voice. "How about never? Is never good for you?"

She spun on her heel and stormed out of the office, slamming the door behind her. She didn't even slow down when she heard the glass in the door shatter.

In fact, Kat didn't slow down long enough to put on her coat until she was out of the building and nearly three blocks away.

Kat stood on the street corner and growled under her breath. She was already well past the point where she'd had enough of this nonsense. Half of her interviews so far had gone exactly like this one. If it wasn't computer whiz-kids barely older than herself who couldn't get over being in a room with someone who was (as one of them put it) "even hotter than Lara Croft," then it was balding, paunchy personnel directors mired in mid-life crises. Kat had neither the desire nor the intention to take a job where her chief qualification was as someone's fantasy object.

Yet, in the other half of her interviews, Kat kept facing the exact problem that Ms. Mickel had predicted back at the employment agency. The long and the short of it was that Kat had no relevant work experience. In fact, other than summers at the Kwikee Burger back home, she had no work experience at all. She hadn't finished her degree, and hadn't even made it halfway through the coursework for her major in computer science by the time I.O. whisked her away from school.

Finally, and perhaps most ironically when you considered her age, a lot of the computer knowledge Kat had acquired at Princeton was already growing outdated. The technology was changing at light speed. The evolution was racing forward so quickly that, over the course of the time she'd spent with Gen[13], new generations of hardware and programming languages were already beginning to appear. They were displacing the stuff Kat had learned to take over the mantle of "cutting-edge."

At her age, it wasn't easy for Kat to think of herself as obsolete. But when you put it all together, it didn't exactly position Kat as the ideal candidate for a job.

Kat stood there for a bit, just watching the steam that came from her breath in the winter air. When she felt a little more calm, she hiked up her sleeve and looked at her watch.

One-thirty already? she thought with surprise. *Where'd the day go?*

Kat took out her schedule of interviews and checked it again, even though she had it virtually memorized. A glance confirmed that, as she had thought, her next interview was nearby, and it wasn't scheduled to start until two o'clock.

Kat decided to take advantage of the opportunity to grab a little lunch and recover from the blur of waiting rooms, interviews, circling and crossing out want ads, and dropping off resumes. She wasn't especially familiar with the neighborhood down here in Tribeca. The area was harder to navigate than the bulk of the City that stretched uptown. The streets down here had names instead of sequential numbers, and some of the streets veered off at odd angles instead of maintaining a boxlike grid like most of Manhattan. Even down here, though, Kat knew that it was difficult to throw a stone in Manhattan without hitting a deli of some kind. Sure enough, when she looked around, she discovered one less than a block away.

Kat walked inside and headed straight for the salad bar. As she rummaged through the bar and made her selections, Kat took stock of her situation.

Clearly, finding the right job wasn't going to be as easy as she had hoped. In many ways, searching for a job felt a lot like an endless series of blind dates, complete with all the nervousness and potential for rejection that analogy implied. And just as in blind dating, there was no way to know how long the process would have to continue before she found "Mister Right."

Kat's hand stopped halfway toward the bin of sliced tomatoes, hovering above the salad bar as she was struck by a troubling thought. What if she *never* found the right job? There were no guarantees that she ever would. Would she just have to give up? If not, what would she wind up having to settle for?

There was no way around the fact that the search was going to be hard. She'd known that from the start, much as she'd tried not to think about it. The real question was whether the ultimate payoff would be worth it. Unlike most of the other people searching for jobs out there, Kat didn't really have to work. Mister Lynch covered the living expenses for all of Gen¹³, and gave each of them a generous weekly allowance besides. She had a gorgeous place to live, and more than enough pocket money for her modest needs.

But, as Sarah had pointed out to the others, that wasn't why Kat was looking for a job. Kat didn't need this for the money. She needed it for herself. And that, she realized with a deep sigh, wasn't something that was going to go away anytime soon.

So yes, she figured, the search was worth it. It wasn't going to be easy, but it was worth it.

Kat paid for her salad and took it outside to sit on the bench at a bus stop while she ate. She sat alone on the corner, fighting to eat her salad before the wind blew too much of it away. The solitary, outdoor meal wasn't the most lavish she'd ever eaten, nor was it the most enjoyable. After spending hours mired in the looking-for-work grind, there was a big part of her that wished she could be off with her friends instead.

Kat wondered what the others were doing right now. She bet it was something fun.

Roxanne lay on her stomach, sprawled sideways across her bed. She was dressed now, but that wasn't the most distinctive thing about how she looked. No, the distinctive thing was her eyes, which were puffy and red with tears.

Despite all the things Roxy did to make herself appear older—the attitude, the cigarettes, the tank tops and miniskirts—she was still, in many ways, not much more than a little girl. Roxy worked hard to project a tough outer shell, but most of it was an act—a mask to protect the sensitive, insecure soul beneath.

What's wrong with me? she asked herself.

Roxy tried so hard to get close to people. She really did. But time after time, it always turned out the same way: Just when it looked like she'd succeeded ... just when she'd start to feel comfortable ... the other person would push her away.

She thought about how hard she'd worked to land Grunge as her boyfriend. For the longest time, no matter what she did, it seemed like he barely realized she was alive. Or if he did notice her, it was more like a friend or sister thing than hearts and flowers. He was too interested in silicone babes with bodies like blow-up dolls ... and brains to match.

Then, one day, for no reason at all, it just clicked. Everything fell into place, and Grunge looked at her like he'd never really seen her before. And all of a sudden, Roxy's unrequited love wasn't unrequited anymore. The harps were playing. The angels were singing. Roxy was walking on air—and without even using her powers.

Except that it took less than a day for Grunge's wandering eye to start wandering again.

It wasn't that he'd been unfaithful to her. For one thing, no matter how much Grunge might like to window shop, Roxy knew that he wouldn't ever take things that far. He was a dog, sure, but he wouldn't do that to her. And besides, he knew full well that, if he ever did take it too far, Roxy would make sure that it would never be physically possible for him to do it again.

But even if all he was doing was looking, it still hurt. It hurt to see Grunge drooling over every other woman on Earth.

Because it meant Roxy wasn't enough.

And while Roxy never imagined that Kat had it in her to hurt someone like that, it was starting to look like the same kind of thing was happening all over again. After all these years of feeling alone, after all these years of praying for someone who would stand by her side no matter what, Roxy discovered that she had a sister. Okay, technically, she was a half-sister, but still—a sister! The nicest, sweetest, kindest sister anyone could ask for. At last, Roxy had someone to confide in, someone who'd never turn her away.

Or so she thought. Because that's exactly what was happening.

No matter what Kat said, Roxy had a hard time believing that the timing was coincidence. No sooner had Kat discovered that Roxy was her sister, than she suddenly decided she needed to get out of the house more.

Roxy stopped herself. *No*, she admitted silently, *that's not fair*.

Okay, so maybe Roxy wasn't really the reason for

Kat's job hunt. But even so, the fact remained that Kat wasn't satisfied with her life. She was out there looking for a job because she didn't feel like she had enough in her life otherwise. Despite having a newfound sister, Kat didn't feel there was enough in her life to keep her interest.

And that meant Roxy wasn't enough.

Not that she blamed Kat. Kat had brains up the wazoo, and a wazoo that didn't quit. She was smarter than Roxy, prettier than Roxy, stronger than Roxy, nicer than Roxy . . .

So, realistically speaking, what did she need Roxy for?

It wasn't the first time it had happened to Roxy. Growing up, Roxy had never known her real father, Alex Fairchild. Roxy was born of a one-night stand, and if her father ever even knew she existed, he didn't care enough to want to see her. Not even her own father needed her.

Still, there was one person that Roxy knew loved her more than anything, and that was her stepmother. The two of them might have been dirt poor, but her stepmom—her Momma—never once put her own needs before Roxy's. She did whatever she had to do to make sure that Roxy was fed and clothed and had a roof over her head.

And how had Roxy repaid her? With nothing but problems and bad attitude. With twenty-twenty hindsight, Roxy cringed as the arguments kept replaying themselves in her mind.

"I understand how you feel, honey, but—"

"No, Momma! There's no 'but!' You always do that. You just dismiss my feelings! You don't care how I feel!"

"How can you say that? Of course I care about how you feel!"

"Yeah? Then why is there always a 'but?' Why is it always 'I know, but . . . ?' Why can't you just listen to me for once?"

"You think you're the only one who feels that way? You think you're the only one who wants the other person

to listen sometimes? When's the last time you paid attention to how I was feeling?"

"Look, I don't need any of this right now. I'm going out . . . "

The thing was, Roxy loved her stepmother every bit as much as her Momma loved her. Even when they were fighting and screaming at their worst, that never changed. Way down in the roots of her soul, Roxy knew that.

But did her Momma know?

For probably the millionth time, Roxy wondered whether her juvenile, immature mouthing off had pushed her stepmother away.

The last time Roxy had seen her mother was just before she left for the "special school" that was really a front for I.O.'s Gen[13] program. Her stepmother seemed so proud of her for getting recruited to such an exclusive school. Maybe even prouder than Roxy herself. She wrote letters every day, although Roxy, of course, was too cool to spend time writing letters back to her mother.

Was that the final straw? Maybe it was.

Because by the time Roxy got her powers, busted out of the facility with the rest of Gen[13], and tried to get in touch with her Momma, her Momma was gone. Roxy's stepmother had packed up, left the apartment, and moved on. And not just once, either. When Roxy tried to trace her Momma's forwarding address, she discovered that her Momma had moved a bunch of times—so many that Roxy had begun to wonder whether she even wanted Roxy to find her in the first place. Roxy's latest lead placed her stepmother right here in New York. So far, though, Roxy still hadn't worked up the nerve to check.

Her Momma had been the one person in the world who truly loved Roxy. And Roxy had screwed the whole thing up.

If you wanted to get honest about it, that was why she started taking on the whole attitude in the first place. That was why she always pushed people away.

Because she didn't want to give them the chance to

realize that she wasn't worth it. Deep down, her greatest fear was that they'd leave her first.

There was a knock at the door.

"Go away," Roxy said.

The knock came again, gentler this time.

"I said, go away!"

The door cracked open, and Grunge tentatively stuck his head inside. There was a look of concern on his face. "Babe? Are you okay?" Grunge asked. "The Bobster said you were acting all, like, weird before . . ."

"I'm fine," she said, turning her head to hide her puffy eyes.

"Fine."

"Yeah, fine."

"No, you're not."

"Oh, what do you care?"

Grunge reacted to that one with genuine surprise. "What do I care?" He stepped the rest of the way into the room and closed the door. "I care 'cause you're my sweetie. I care 'cause if this was all the other way around and stuff, and I was the one all like that, then you'd care."

Grunge sat down on the bed beside her. "I care," he said, in a gentler tone than Roxy had ever heard him use before, "because I care about you."

"Oh, Grunge . . ."

Roxy sat up and threw her arms around him. They sat like that for a while, not saying anything. Just holding each other tightly.

Then, they kissed.

The entire apartment was rocked by a massive explosion.

"Whoa," said Grunge. "Was it good for you?"

"Come on!" exclaimed Roxy. She had already snapped out of her mood and was literally flying from the bed to the door to see what was wrong.

They hurried into the hall. The smoke and dust was billowing in from the living room.

"This way!" said Grunge. But there was no need. Roxy was already ahead of him.

The pair ran into the living room to find that the broken doorknob on the front door was no longer an issue. Because there was no longer a front door.

Or a wall around it.

The dust from the rubble hadn't settled yet. It filled the air, making it hard to breathe without coughing.

Yet, there, amidst the debris, stood Bobby and Sarah, poised for battle. Roxy hadn't known what to expect, but even so, her first glimpse of their attackers took her by surprise. (And for a member of a super-team who'd recently fought a bunch of mind-controlled lingerie models, that was saying something.)

Standing opposite Sarah and Bobby were ten grim, unblinking foes. Each of them was clothed in a matching black, skintight uniform. Each of them was no more than twelve years old. And despite their combat-ready stances, each of them wore an impassive, almost bored expression.

Grunge laughed. "What's this," he said, "the Jailbait League of America?"

A cute girl with close-cut hair and an upturned nose stood at the front of the pack. She looked at Grunge as though he was something she might possibly deign to scrape off her shoe. "If you absolutely must call us something," she said, "it would be preferable for you to use our established code name:

"*Gen^{14}!*"

CHAPTER 8

It had been a long day. By the time Kat got up to her second to last job interview, she felt like she'd gone six rounds with a giant robot. And as someone who'd gone six rounds with giant robots on more than one occasion, she knew what she was talking about.

Kat was tired. She was frustrated. Her super-strong feet hurt.

How did regular people do this all the time?

Kat stood in front of the building where her next interview was scheduled. Many of the office and apartment buildings down here in Soho had been converted from warehouses long ago. This one still looked like it, a long brick building that wasn't particularly tall by New York standards—only about four or five stories—but that took up most of the block. Her appointment was on the top floor.

Kat blew the hair out of her eyes, and took another look at the schedule in her hand:

"3:00 PM—Girlsworld.com"

"Girlsworld," huh? Kat thought. *Well, doing something with girls would be fun. Maybe this one'll be different.*

But with the way my luck's been running today, she continued, *they probably manufacture 3-D cybersex.*

The members of Gen[13] looked at each other, puzzled.

" 'Gen-*four*teen?' " Roxy wondered. "Wouldn't that make them *our kids?*"

Grunge recoiled and thrust out his palms protectively. "Whoa!" he said. "Don't look at me!"

"Anybody put out a call for a junior fan club?" Bobby said.

"Now, wait a minute. This is ridiculous," said Sarah. She turned to the blonde girl who'd spoken. "Look, I don't know how you guys did that to the wall, but we're not going to fight a bunch of kids. Why don't you all just go home, and we'll forget this ever happened?"

"Reverb," said the blonde girl.

Without warning, one of the boys raised his hands in Sarah's direction. The air was split by a loud *THRUMMMMM*. Despite the considerable distance between them—and the fact that there was nothing visible bridging the gap—Sarah was knocked clear across the room.

The effect on both groups was electrifying. The room erupted into a flurry of motion.

As far as the heroes were concerned, the age difference between them no longer mattered. These kids were both powerful and dangerous. They had to be stopped—a little more gently than usual, perhaps—but quickly, before it was too late.

"Slash, Override, go," the blonde girl said without emotion. "Riptide, Growing Boy, go. Rave, Sidestep, go. Knockout, Reverb, on back-up and watch for Fairchild. Bogeyman, with me. Go."

Bobby soared up toward the ceiling, his body a mass of flame. Even without his costume, you couldn't really call him Bobby Lane anymore. He was Burnout now.

They're organized, Burnout thought. *So taking out their leader should make a difference.* He prepared to hurl a firebolt, but as the mass of superheated plasma swelled to fill his palm, he hesitated. Burnout didn't have it in him to set fire to a twelve-year-old girl. So he chose to go with a different option. It would take more control to ignite the rug around her and pen her in, but at least that way, he wouldn't cause any serious injury. Burnout took careful aim and let fly.

The blast never hit the mark. Burnout was shocked to see one boy's arm dissolve into a powerful jet of water. The water spout shot forth to intercept the fiery projectile in a sizzling cloud of steam.

"*Riptide!*" Burnout thought. Before he could react, Riptide's entire upper body transformed into a gushing river of water that surged up to hit him with the force of a riot hose. The rush of water slammed Burnout against the ceiling, extinguishing his flame and knocking him silly, before subsiding to become Riptide's human form once again. Dazed and soaking wet, it took all of Burnout's concentration to summon up enough of a meager, sputtering flame to maintain the thermal updraft that held him aloft.

Which is part of the reason why he was surprised to feel a tap on his shoulder.

He turned. One of the other boys was standing behind him. Not flying, Burnout realized. The kid was *standing*. Growing Boy was now so massive that he had to crouch in order to stand beneath the living room's fifteen-foot ceiling. And more than that, Burnout saw something else:

A giant fist coming straight at him.

The fist connected in a shattering blow that sent Burnout crashing to the floor below.

Fighting to stay conscious, Burnout looked up to see his towering foe disappear. "Where . . . ?" Burnout started to say.

As soon as Burnout opened his mouth, he felt something jump inside. Something that moved on his tongue. Something alive.

Gagging with disgust, Burnout tried to spit out the foreign object. But before he had the chance, he screamed. An excruciating pressure was forcing itself simultaneously against his jaw and the roof of his mouth.

Growing Boy was inside Burnout's mouth.

And he was starting to grow.

. . .

For her part, Roxy—or, more precisely in the heat of battle, Freefall—didn't hesitate when she saw the blonde girl who led Gen[14] leaping toward her. Freefall gestured, canceling out the gravity beneath the girl, so that the leap sent her flying over Freefall's head and into the wall behind her.

What Freefall didn't expect was what happened next. The girl spun around in mid-leap and bent her knees to absorb the shock of impact with her legs. Without so much as a split-second pause, the girl sprang back off the wall, using the momentum to propel her upward as she somersaulted again to hit the ceiling with her feet. She thrust her feet out forcefully against the ceiling. The move doubled her momentum, sending her hurtling downward at breathtaking speed—straight at Freefall.

The entire maneuver had taken no more than a second or two. It was almost too fast for Freefall to follow, let alone ready a defense. All Freefall could do was try to dodge.

Freefall managed to get partially out of the way, so that the girl struck her only a glancing blow, before using her hands to turn the fall into a rolling series of flips that cushioned the landing. But with Freefall off-balance due to her evasive move, even a glancing blow was enough to knock her off her feet.

Even as she hit the floor, Freefall knew what she had to do. Instead of negating gravity, she had to quadruple it and pin her agile opponent to the floor. The girl was moving so fast, though, that it was hard to get a bead on her. Time after time, freefall shot out a rapid-fire series of heavy-gravity fields, but time after time, she missed.

The effort wasn't wasted, though. Each time, Freefall got a little closer. She was starting to home in . . .

"Highwire, clear!" shouted the girl's partner, a towheaded boy.

The girl did a quick backflip away from Freefall.

And suddenly, all of the Gen[14] kids were gone.

Freefall looked around, confused. Her teammates looked equally surprised. But they were the only ones there.

"Huh?" she said. "Where'd they go?"

Wincing, Sarah picked herself up off the floor. "I don't know. I guess we drove them off," she said. "No thanks to you."

Roxy did a double-take. "Wh-what?"

"Yeah," Bobby agreed. Painfully, he rose to his knees, then his feet. "I mean, a little girl who bounces around a lot? And you can't even stop her?" He shaped his fingers into an L and pressed them to his forehead. "What a loser."

"Now-now, wait a minute!" Roxy said. "Don't blame me! She was really fast!"

"Oh, forgive me," Sarah said, rolling her eyes. "I see. She was fast. I somehow neglected to notice how fast she was, seeing as how *I* was getting blasted across the room at the time."

"Hey! What's up with you guys? Come on, cut me a little slack here!"

"Don't sweat it, Rox," Grunge said, as he picked bits of rubble out of his long hair. "The guys just lose it a little sometimes, what with you being the weak link and all."

Roxy was stunned. "W-weak link . . . ?"

"Yeah, you know. It's not like it's a surprise or anything, right?"

"B-but . . ."

"I mean, lookit," he continued. "There's Bobby shootin' out fire all over the place. And Sarah—well, she's got this whole weather thing going on. Whoof. And Kat's all, like, super-amazon chick, punching out tanks with the bullets bouncin' off her. And there I am, turning into bricks and solid steel and junk.

"And you? You make things light and heavy. It's cute, but when we're really throwin' down with somebody, well, it's just not in the same class, y'know?"

Roxy felt like the floor had dropped out from beneath her. Grunge wasn't saying anything that she hadn't always suspected herself. None of them were. But to hear it from their own mouths . . .

"Is—is that what you really think?" Roxy asked Grunge. "Is that what you *all* think?"

Grunge shrugged. "Sorry, babe. We didn't want to say anything before. We were keepin' it on the down low, because, y'know, we felt sorry for you."

". . . S-sorry . . . ?"

"Yeah. Kinda like why I was dating you and all."

Roxy tried to speak. But she couldn't think of anything to say.

"But nothin' lasts forever, right? I mean, geez, you wouldn't even put out."

Roxy could feel her lower lip quivering, as Kat leaned in close. (Had Kat been there a minute ago?) Kat spoke quietly, her face scrunched up at the awkwardness of the situation. "I'm sorry you had to find out like this, Roxy. But now that you know. . . . Well, maybe it would be better for everyone in the long run if you just left now."

"K-Kat . . . ? . . . B-but you're my sister!"

Kat winced. "Oh, right. That's another thing. In the future, would you mind . . .

". . . you know . . .

". . . not mentioning that to anyone?"

The tears were starting to flow down Roxy's cheeks now.

"I don't want to hurt your feelings or anything But you know how it is, right?" Kat said, with a little shrug and a knowing nod. "Thanks."

Kat gave her a little pat on the shoulder and joined the others. With a final look of pity, they turned and started to walk away.

It was getting dark.

"W-wait!" Roxy yelled after them, sobbing. "H-how can you treat me like this?! How can you be so cruel?!"

A mirthless chuckle came from behind her. "Now, there's a joke."

Roxy turned to look at the speaker through her tears. It was a thin woman, a little more than twice Roxy's age. Her eyes were a striking shade of green; her hair a sandy brown that had once been natural but now was helped along by regularly scheduled dye jobs to hide the gray. Her sunken cheeks and the lines that criss-crossed her forehead hinted at a life that hadn't been easy. She took a long drag on a cigarette as Roxy let the shock of recognition sink in.

"M-Momma . . . ?" Roxy said.

Sure enough, her stepmother was sitting on the sofa with arms crossed and a disapproving air about her. "You're a fine one to complain. After the way you treated me?"

Roxy fell to her knees and threw herself at her stepmother's feet. "Oh, Momma! I didn't mean it! Any of it! I'm so, so sorry!"

"Too late for that, kid. Much too late."

Roxy's stepmother brushed her away and stood over her. The color drained from Roxy's tear-streaked face as she looked pleadingly up at her. "To tell you the truth," her stepmother continued, "I should probably thank you. Sure, it was hard at first. When you left, and then when you never returned my letters, it hurt.

"But after a while, I realized something—something that changed my life.

"With you gone, I was free! I was completely, totally free! I could go wherever I wanted. I could do whatever I wanted. For the first time in years, there was nothing to drag me down like a lead weight around my neck."

Instinctively, Roxy started to pull in her arms and legs, and curl into a ball. ". . . B-but, M-Momma . . . ," she murmured quietly, ". . . I . . . I love you . . ."

"Yeah, well, I used to think I did, too. It passes."

". . . Momma . . . please . . ."

Her stepmother gave a huff. She bent down to look

Roxy straight in the eye—or she would, if Roxy's eyes
weren't already shut tight. "Listen, Roxanne, this may be
tough for you to hear, but it's for your own good. So pay
attention for once.

"You were a mistake. Your parents didn't want you.
Nobody wanted you. The only one who was even willing
to tolerate you was me, and I was wrong.

"I'm *glad* you left! To tell you the truth, I wish you'd
never shown up in the first place! You ruined my life!"

She leaned in close to hiss the clincher:

"I'm sorry you were ever born!"

From the depths of her soul, Roxy screamed.

"Nnnnooooooooooooo!"

Roxy's howl cut through the raucous din of battle like
a knife.

"Rox!" yelled Grunge. He looked away from his own
foe to see Roxy curled up in a fetal position at the feet
of the towheaded kid, the one they called Bogeyman.

He turned back to face Slash, whose arms had transformed into a pair of menacing blades that shone like
razor-sharp scimitars. "*Wicked* mistake, dudes!" Grunge
snarled. "I *was* gonna take it easy on you, seein' as how
you're kids and all. But messin' with my sweetie crosses
the line!"

Grunge grabbed hold of his bronze belt buckle. Instantly, his hand began to change, taking on the gleaming
brownish-yellow appearance and texture of the buckle itself. The effect spread up his arm, across his shoulders,
and down his chest and back, until his entire body completed the change. He looked more like a living statue
than a human being—a living statue that was mad.

"Say your prayers! 'Cause there's a half ton of mad
metal in your face, and I got more important things than
you to take care of!"

With a roar, Grunge leaped to the attack. Slash
matched his charge. Slash thrusted and whirled, employ-
ing his blades with such grace that the fierce offensive

almost resembled a dance. The air hummed with each pass of the blades, and each contact resounded with the sound of metal on metal. Grunge parried and blocked the blows with single-minded determination, using his arms and shoulders to protect his face. It was a defense that would have left a normal man dismembered, but thanks to Grunge's bronze form, each blow did little more than shave off ribbons of metal in a small shower of sparks.

It was a mark of Grunge's concern for Roxy that he wasn't even bothering to indulge his usual non-stop stream of patter. Wordlessly, Grunge moved in closer, wading through the hail of blows. He raised his fist to deliver the finale . . .

. . . and froze.

It wasn't just Grunge's arm, either. His whole body was paralyzed. He tried to move his legs, but they wouldn't respond. Nor would his hands or neck or anything else. Grunge couldn't even move his tongue and lips to speak, or his eyes to see what was going on. He had become the bronze statue he resembled.

It was a bizarre sensation. As Grunge tried to will his body to move, he didn't feel any strain or resistance, as though something was holding him back. Instead, he simply felt . . . nothing. It was as though his body had become disconnected from his brain. As though his body had simply stopped working.

Slash just watched him, passively, without so much as a sneer of triumph. Grunge didn't get it. How was Slash doing this?

Then he realized Slash wasn't. Out of the corner of his eye, Grunge spotted one of the girls facing him. She was standing motionless despite the battle raging throughout the room, her eyes closed.

What'd that blonde chick call her? Grunge thought. *"Overdrive?"*

Then it came to him. He would have slapped himself in the forehead for overlooking the obvious if he could. *No,* he thought. *"Override."*

Just then, Grunge started to move again.

You'd think he would have been happy about it. After all, that was precisely what he'd been trying to do, just a moment ago, with no success.

But he wasn't happy about it. Because he wasn't doing it.

Grunge watched helplessly as he put one foot in front of the other and slowly started to walk. It was like being a passenger in his own body. He tried to stop himself, but he had as little luck preventing the action as he'd had when he was the one trying to initiate it.

Grunge's heavy bronze arms raised themselves high over his head. His hands clasped together in a double fist.

Grunge's mind recoiled in horror as he suddenly realized what his body was about to do. He was about to bring his hands down in a devastating blow that would smash the target at his feet to pulp.

And the target at his feet was Roxy.

Rainmaker didn't know how the kid had done it, but whatever it was, she'd hit the far wall of the living room hard. The pain in her side was terrible, and it hurt more whenever she moved. Rainmaker suspected that the impact had at least cracked, if not broken, a rib or two.

She couldn't afford the luxury of taking time to recover, though. Despite the pain, she forced herself to her feet and prepared to use her own powers to retaliate.

Before she could, though, the world went mad.

The last coherent thing Rainmaker could remember was Rave's eyes narrowing. Then Rainmaker's senses erupted. Her head starting spinning violently. Everything around her dissolved into a swirling mass of light and color with no distinguishable shape or form. Her ears were filled with howling, surging waves of sound, as though someone had recorded a random symphony of noise—and then played it backward. Her tongue tasted loud, and the world felt purple. Rainmaker had no idea which way was up. She couldn't tell where her body ended and everything else began. The cacophony of disjointed sensation filled her head to bursting. She was afraid even to move for fear of falling over . . . assuming that she hadn't already.

Rainmaker thought she screamed. But she couldn't be sure.

The strategy was perfect, serving simultaneously as both attack and defense. Calling it overwhelming would have been the understatement of the century. And at the same time, there was no way to launch a counterattack, or even defend herself. She couldn't possibly risk using her own powers. As it was, she could barely manage linear thought. If she tried to command the weather with her senses running amok, there was as much chance of doing damage to one of her friends as one of her foes. She might even wind up striking herself.

Then, without warning, it stopped.

Rainmaker staggered and sagged, her body so thoroughly exhausted from the ordeal that a massive hangover would have been a step up. She grabbed onto the nearby window moulding to keep from falling. But while every neuron in her body felt like it had been stretched past its limits and twisted in knots, she was grateful. At least, she could see and hear again. Of course, it meant that the searing pain in her side had returned, too, but at this point, she had to be grateful for small favors.

Rainmaker's mind was racing. She just didn't get it. Admittedly, she was still having trouble thinking straight, but Rave's strategy didn't make any sense. Why would Rave stop now? Why not finish Sarah off first?

Rainmaker squinted through her disheveled hair to see Sidestep watching her. A small patch of air in front of Sidestep was shimmering. Rainmaker stared, curious, as Sidestep reached her arm out in Rainmaker's direction. But as Sidestep's hand and forearm met the shimmering patch, they disappeared into nothingness.

Suddenly, Rainmaker's entire body was wracked with a evel of agony that dwarfed the pain she felt in her side.

She went pale. She couldn't breathe. A terrible pressure engulfed her heart.

Rainmaker sank to the floor. Her head smacked against the metal of the sputtering baseboard heater. But she didn't even notice the pain of impact or the heat.

Oh, God! she thought. *I'm—I'm having a heart attack! It's like someone's hand squeezing my heart!*

Slowly—

Like someone's . . . hand . . .

—the light—

. . . squeezing . . .

—started to dawn—

. . . my heart . . .

—and Rainmaker realized the truth.

. . . My . . . God . . .

Her hand's . . . inside me . . .

That was it.

That was why Rave had released her.

They didn't just want to kill her.

They wanted her to feel it, too.

CHAPTER 9

B urnout knew he had to act fast. The pressure inside his mouth was mounting. He had only seconds left before Growing Boy's size would increase enough to tear off Burnout's jaw and rip his head apart.

But what could he do? He was still soaking wet from Riptide's attack. It didn't stop him from using his powers, but it hampered them a whole lot.

Growing Boy was getting bigger. As he started to fill Burnout's mouth and throat, Burnout felt himself gag. He had to fight not to throw up.

No! he thought. *That's it!*

Burnout was soaking wet . . .

. . . but only on the outside.

Burnout let the heat build within his stomach. He was still gagging, but now he welcomed the feeling. Because it was going to save his life.

Growing Boy felt the heat, too. The rising temperature took a moment to catch his attention, but once it did, he quickly realized what it meant.

Growing Boy was too big now to escape Burnout's mouth. Quickly, he started to shrink back down.

Burnout's stomach convulsed. A ball of fiery plasma coursed up his throat and out his mouth. Growing Boy leaped from Burnout's mouth less than a second ahead of the flames. If they had caught him full-on, he would have been burned to a crisp. He avoided that fate by a hairsbreadth, but he was still too close to the wave of fire to come out of it unscathed.

As the minuscule assassin put as much distance as he could between his intended victim and himself, Burnout bent over the arm of the sofa, retching up bits of flame that smoldered on the carpet. Panting and sweating, he extinguished the tiny fires with his foot, and looked up . . .

. . . to see Grunge about to smash Freefall.

Unable to fly, Burnout ran as fast as his weakened condition would allow, and flung himself at his best friend. Grunge was so heavy in his bronze form that a standard flying tackle aimed at his waist would have had no effect. But Burnout wasn't aiming for Grunge's waist.

Reared back for the blow, with his arms held high over his head, Grunge was already off-balance. Burnout grabbed onto Grunge's hands, and with the full force of his weight, tipped his metallic teammate backwards. The floor shook as Grunge landed on his back with a crash.

Still unable to speak, Grunge silently cheered his friend on.

Burnout scrambled to his feet, searching to see if Sarah needed help, too. But he wouldn't get the chance.

Because when he looked around, Burnout saw a twelve-year-old girl grabbing Grunge by the ankles and hoisting him off the floor. Knockout spun around, swinging Grunge at Burnout like a giant, five-foot metal club.

Grunge managed to start the change back to flesh and bone before he connected. But he still couldn't move and still couldn't stop the impact. There was a sickening thud as the semi-bronze hero connected with his friend. Burnout was knocked clear off his feet.

Knockout casually tossed Grunge off to the side. He landed on—or, more accurately, through—a coffee table that shattered beneath his weight. With no visible show of emotion, she moved in toward Burnout to finish him off.

Rainmaker gritted her teeth against the pain. She had to do something. She couldn't just give up and die.

But what could she do? The white-hot agony that filled

115

her body prevented her from so much as standing up. She could try to use her powers against Sidestep from a distance, but with her hand inside Rainmaker's chest, the chances were good that she'd just wind up killing herself. If she hit Sidestep with a bolt of lightning, it was the same as blasting it straight into her own heart.

There was no point to counting on any help from her teammates, either. Fighting against her own reflexes, Rainmaker forced her eyes open long enough to see that they weren't doing any better against Gen[14] than she was. If something, or someone, didn't turn the tables quickly, they were all dead.

Where were Lynch and Kat? It was bad enough that Gen[13] was so badly outpowered. But in the face of a well-organized enemy, they were leaderless, too.

Rainmaker could see only one answer. And she was the only one who could execute it.

The only option Rainmaker could see was to push her control of the elements further than ever before. She could sweep the room with the combined force of a blizzard, a hailstorm, and a full-blown hurricane. No one could survive all of that for long. It was a last-ditch solution, one that was likely to cost her life . . . and the lives of her friends as well.

But the odds were that it would kill Gen[14], too.

We're dead anyway, she told herself through the pain. *These kids are too dangerous. They're inhuman. They could slaughter millions—and they will.*

Unless it ends here.

Rainmaker said a silent prayer. She bid goodbye to her friends. She prepared herself to do what she had to do.

It's funny the sorts of things that go through your mind at a time like that. Despite the pain, despite the roar of battle all around her, all Rainmaker could hear was the sputtering of the heater beside her ear.

Suddenly, Rainmaker's eyes opened wide. *The heater!*

Rainmaker gave a quick mental command. Out of nowhere, a massive bolt of lightning shot down from the sky to blast the wall near the heater. The plaster shattered. The pipes within the wall burst, releasing powerful, billowing jets of scalding hot steam.

Sidestep jumped back to avoid it, and the pressure in Rainmaker's chest was gone. Rainmaker could see her own blood on Sidestep's hand.

But only for a moment.

Within seconds, the clouds of steam filled the room, making it impossible to see anything. Rainmaker was still trembling, and battling to stave off shock and unconsciousness. Yet, she realized her makeshift smoke screen wouldn't hold off their opponents forever. She had bought herself only a small margin, and she needed to make the most of it.

Ironically, Rainmaker's greatest advantage was that her team was already down on the floor, where the steam wasn't quite as thick. All she had to do was summon up a mild breeze to clear a small zone of visibility around her, while the Gen[14] kids groped around blindly.

Highwire's commanding voice cut through the mist. "Where'd they go?" she called. "Sweep the room! Sing out when you find one of them!"

Mustering up her remaining strength, Rainmaker crawled quickly beneath the steam. Every movement brought new agony to her broken rib. But still, she pushed on until she reached the spot where Grunge was already stirring. He shook his head to clear it, his long hair flying.

"Tssst!" Rainmaker hissed.

Grunge brushed the hair from his face, a determined look in his eyes. "Where's Rox?" he whispered back.

Rainmaker increased the breeze slightly but kept it near the floor. As more of the area cleared, Freefall came into view. She was still curled up in a ball, her eyes tightly closed.

Rainmaker cupped her hands to Grunge's ear to minimize the odds of their being overheard. "We've got to get out of here," Rainmaker whispered. "You grab Roxy and get her to safety. I'll go after Bobby."

"Right."

"And stay low. Take the fire stairs. If we get separated, I'll meet you out back in the alley."

With a quick nod, Grunge headed off.

Even as she made her own way toward Burnout, Rainmaker had to marvel. She'd never seen Grunge with so little to say before.

He really does *love her*, she thought.

Moving forward, Rainmaker was surprised to see Burnout already crawling toward her in a clear zone of his own. Apparently, they'd had the same idea, though she didn't know how he'd managed it. Then, as he came closer, she felt the wave of heat and figured it out. He was using the same trick that he'd used yesterday in the snow, raising his body heat enough to disperse the steam around him.

Burnout's way was riskier, though. Because if one of the Gen[14] kids felt the sudden rise in temperature as he passed, they'd be able to pinpoint his location.

Rainmaker drew a finger across her throat, signalling him to cut the heat. Burnout nodded. She pointed toward the door, then set off toward it. Burnout followed close behind.

The door seemed miles away. But they covered the distance swiftly.

As they headed out into the hall, Sarah looked back at the remains of their beautiful apartment.

This isn't over, she thought grimly.

It took several minutes for Knockout to follow the sound of hissing steam back to its source and feel her way to the broken pipes. Then, after she crushed the pipes to slow the billowing steam to a trickle, it still took several more for the air to clear.

By that time, no one was surprised to see that Gen[13] was gone.

Highwire looked around with a clinical eye. She nodded at the empty apartment without disappointment, as though acknowledging exactly what she had expected to find.

"Mission abort," she said. "Someone is bound to have heard the noise and called the authorities. We cannot risk public exposure at this time.

"Sidestep, withdraw to base."

Sidestep responded with a nod. She began to create the teleportational portal they'd need.

"What about Fairchild?" asked Reverb. "Intel indicated a fifth member of Gen^{13}."

"The other targets are likely to alert her," Highwire answered. "In all probability, they know where she is. We do not."

While Highwire had been talking, Riptide had been surveying the area around him. Mostly, it was just the shattered remains of objects that had been broken in the fight. However, his interest was piqued by a sheet of paper lying on the bar next to him. The thing that caught his eye was Caitlin Fairchild's name, printed in bold letters across the top of the page. He scanned the sheet, which was limp from the steam, but still perfectly legible. Gingerly, he peeled the wilted resume off the bar and turned it over. The back was covered with a list of times, names, and telephone numbers.

"Perhaps we do know where she is," Riptide said.

It's worth it, Kat thought. *All of it.*

Everything that Kat had put up with all day long faded into the background. In the half-hour since she'd arrived at the converted loft that housed the company, it was as though everything that Kat had endured in her other interviews had ceased to exist.

". . . So I was reading the American Association of University Women report," the woman was saying, "and it just sort of clicked in my head. Here you've got thousands and thousands of teenage young women dropping out of science and technology, right? So what struck me all a sudden is that, after a while, it starts to turn into a self-fulfilling prophecy. The technology doesn't attract women because it isn't designed to appeal to women."

"Because it's been built by men."

"Exactly! Most of the girls drop out before they grow up to design stuff themselves, so they're not around to build the next generation technology. So when the next set of girls comes down the pike, what do they find?"

"More of the same."

"And that's not going to draw them in any more than it did the last time around. To really engage them, you need stuff that's been designed with them in mind. It can't be macho shoot-'em-up games where you think with your testosterone. It needs to feel different, it needs to look different, it needs to be relational instead of coldly logical. It needs to 'think' like they think."

"I get it—you need to invite them in instead of closing them out."

"Right! You need to tear down all the basic assumptions that nobody thinks about but that wind up sitting there like a flashing neon sign that says, 'Boys' club—no girls allowed!' "

"That makes so much sense."

"Well, obviously, it's not the whole answer to getting girls into technology. You've got to remember there are also tiny, little contributing factors like, oh, say, puberty and self-image. It's a start, though. If Girlsworld.com can provide girls with positive, welcoming experiences with technology and pull them into an online community of other girls who are doing the same thing, then we've got a shot at having a real impact. With a little luck, and a whole lot of work, we might just get it right. If we do, then maybe we can empower girls and make a difference."

Kat liked Dorothy Levin. She liked her a lot.

The founder and president of Girlsworld.com didn't look much older than Kat herself. Judging from the masters' degree from M.I.T. that hung on the wall, Dorothy was somewhere in her late twenties. She was constantly talking with her hands, in animated style that reflected a boundless energy to match her commitment. She genuinely cared about the work she did, and her enthusiasm was infectious. Kat had no trouble understanding how Dorothy had managed to wrangle a generous pot of start-up money out of everyone from venture capitalists to the National Science Foundation.

Kat and Dorothy had hit it off almost from the moment Kat walked in. The woman truly wanted to give girls a chance, and Kat got the sense that she took the same approach toward the people who worked for her.

In fact, the small company showed Dorothy's fingerprints all over it. The whole place oozed with a sense of mission that struck a chord deep within Kat. And since most of the staff was female, the sexual politics that felt so overwhelming elsewhere promised to be almost nonexistent here. Every aspect of the place felt exactly like what Kat was looking for.

Best of all, they had an opening for a junior programmer—one that didn't require a whole lot of prior experience.

"To be honest, the job doesn't pay much. But we make up for it with long hours and overwork," Dorothy was saying with a smile. "Seriously, though, there are lots of opportunities to get some great experience, and the people here are terrific."

Kat's ears perked up. Her skin tingled with excitement. This was beginning to sound like a job offer.

"Now, I should warn you," Dorothy continued, "the hours really are long. We pull our fair share of all-nighters and weekends when we have to. But it's worth it.

"I think you'd fit in well here, Kat. What do you say?"

Kat couldn't believe her ears. It was like a dream come true.

And yet . . .

There was also a small voice in the back of Kat's brain that was having second thoughts. Dorothy's mention of long nights and weekends brought back Lynch's concerns about Kat being too inaccessible to the team. What would happen when a crisis conflicted with her deadlines? Kat knew full well that, sooner or later, it was bound to happen. Eventually, one side of her life was going to have to take a back seat to the other.

But still . . . Kat had a rare opportunity here. It seemed much too good to pass up. Maybe she could figure out a way to juggle all of her responsibilities. Maybe she could find a way to make it all work.

Or maybe she was just trying to fool herself.

"Dorothy," Kat said, "I think I'd . . ."

That was when the humming started to build.

Dorothy held up a finger to quiet Kat for a minute. "Do you hear something?" she asked.

Suddenly, the door blew itself off its hinges. The surrounding wall exploded in a hail of bricks, glass, and sound.

Instinctively, Kat threw her invulnerable body over Dorothy to shield her from the debris. She felt chunks of the rubble smash themselves to bits against her back. *Not my good suit!* she thought.

It happened so fast that it wasn't until after the shower of debris subsided that Dorothy even thought to ask: "Wha—what in the . . . ?"

"Sorry," Kat said. "I have a feeling this is for me."

Kat had no idea what this was about, but one of the lessons that Mister Lynch had repeatedly drummed into her head was that finding out could wait until after she'd defended herself and survived. Kat let herself slip into automatic as she straightened and spun toward the source of the blast to assess the situation. As the dust started to clear, she was able to make out a pair of twelve-year-olds, one boy and one girl, standing just past the point where the door once stood. Another girl stood further away, in the middle of the large cubicle area outside Dorothy's office. The shocked employees of Girlsworld.com were cringing against the walls or running for the exit.

Before Kat could react with more than confusion, Reverb struck. This time, though, it wasn't with the sort of devastating blast that had demolished the wall, or even the kind of concussive force that had blown Rainmaker across the room. This was a more subtle gambit, but no less deadly.

Reverb thrust his hand out toward Kat, and her ears filled with a high-pitched whine that cut straight through her brain. As the screech rose even higher in pitch and vibrato, Kat clamped her hands to her ears in pain. It was no use, though. Covering her ears might have muffled the sound entering her ears slightly, but it didn't stop the piercing vibrations from being conducted right through the bone of her skull.

Kat braced herself against the piercing agony and charged Reverb, only to be intercepted by a shuddering blow from Knockout. Knockout caught Kat in the stomach with a fist that could have driven itself through a brick wall without losing momentum. In the past, Kat had faced mortar shells without blinking, but the sucker punch sent her to the floor with the air knocked out of her.

Kat lay there, helpless and gasping. As she struggled to regain her breath and her footing, Knockout delivered a savage kick to her head that laid Kat flat with a grunt. To her utter amazement, Kat felt her lip starting to swell. *But—but that can't be!* Kat thought, even as she instinctively rolled herself into a ball for protection. Kat couldn't remember the last time she'd been injured by a simple kick.

Knockout stomped down on Kat's lower back, directly over her kidneys.

She's . . . strong, Kat thought, through the blinding pain. *Stronger than me.*

To make matters worse, Reverb's sound vibrations showed no sign of easing up. Just the opposite, actually. The vibrations continued to intensify, threatening to turn Kat's brain to jelly. Kat might have had the raw power to go toe to toe with a monster truck, but she was as vulnerable to strokes and aneurysms as anyone else.

Who are *these guys?!* she thought.

Kat knew that she needed to gain some distance. Distance would give her the time she needed to catch her breath, if only for a minute, before bouncing back to launch a counterattack. The problem was that every time she tried to get up, Knockout immediately sent her back down.

And the vibrations were just getting worse.

It was getting harder to think. A dark haze was forming around the edges of her field of vision. Whatever she was going to do, she needed to do it now.

Can't go up . . ., she thought, *but maybe . . .*

Kat rolled over onto her back. Knockout raised her foot for another kick, but before she could bring it down, Kat slammed her fists and feet against the floor with all of her considerable might. The floor was still heavily reinforced from the days when the building served as a warehouse. In those days, every square foot of the floor had to be able to hold several hundred pounds. However, Kat was stronger than that. The reinforced beams within the floor didn't stop it from buckling and giving way under the force of Kat's pounding. Before her adversaries knew what was happening, the floor beneath Kat was gone, and Kat was tumbling down through the hole it left behind.

Directly below, in the offices of Mandl & Pernikoff Actuarial Services, a bespectacled man in a white shirt and bowtie was poring over a mass of ledgers and statistical tables. Kat landed smack in the middle of his desk, shattering it into splinters. She lay there, sprawled in the debris that was once his desk, panting.

The bespectacled man looked down at Kat. He looked around at his scattered papers and the fragments of his desk. He looked back at Kat again and then up.

"Thank you," he murmured to Heaven.

Knockout reacted quickly, jumping to follow Kat down through the hole. But to her surprise, she never made it. In mid-leap, a gale-force wind caught Knockout unawares. The windstorm picked her up like a leaf and hurled her through the glass of a nearby window. In a glistening shower of crystal shards, Knockout sailed out the window and plummeted toward the ground, four stories below.

The sudden appearance of the wind would have been surprising enough. But the most bewildering thing about it was that it had originated indoors.

"Cavalry's here," said Burnout. He leaned his head toward Rainmaker and, as an aside, added, "No offense."

Sarah replied without taking her eyes off Gen^{14}. "On behalf of the entire Apache nation," she said, "none taken."

The four heroes stood near the entrance to the outer office. Usually, the group had an upbeat air about them, but there was no sign of that now. Burnout and Rainmaker stared grimly at the remaining Gen^{14} kids, each poised for battle. Freefall was still clearly shaken, standing huddled in Grunge's arms. And Grunge just looked mad.

The air was filled with a low-pitched roar as Reverb hurled a blast toward them with the speed of sound. But they were ready for him now, and scattered to get out of the way of the offensive a split-second before he let it fly. The vibrations sailed past Gen^{13} and reduced a bank of computer terminals to high-tech dust.

Even as he ducked, Burnout released a ball of fiery plasma that shot toward Reverb. But Reverb was also on the move, so the attack set fire to a bulletin board instead. As Rainmaker summoned a small rain cloud to extinguish the blaze before it grew, Reverb was running toward Sidestep and the shimmering portal that she had created.

"Don't even think it!" Grunge growled, charging after him. Grunge took a running jump toward the fleeing figure, but with inches to spare, Reverb and Sidestep slipped through the portal and were gone. The portal vanished with them, leaving Grunge to slam headfirst into a nearby desk.

Rainmaker stepped cautiously over to the broken window, holding her injured side, and looked down. As she had expected, the super-strong Knockout had survived the fall. Apart from the caved-in roof of an unfortunately parked panel truck, there was no sign of her on the street below.

"They're gone," Sarah said, finally letting her shoulders droop wearily.

"Good thing, too," Burnout replied. "No way are we up for another fight so soon." He drifted gently down through the hole in the floor and landed beside Kat. She was on her feet now, and slowly recovering. She thanked the man in the glasses as he handed her a paper cup full of water.

"You okay?" Burnout asked.

"Wonderful," sighed the man in the glasses.

"I was talking to her."

Kat swallowed the water. Gingerly, she probed her swollen lip with a finger. "Yes, I think so," she replied. "My head's killing me, but I'll live. Thanks for the save."

"Sorry we didn't get here sooner. We had to track down your employment agency to find out where you were."

"You didn't have to do that. I left my schedule in the apartment."

"Yeah, well, that's a whole other story. You're just lucky they only sent the ones who were assigned to take you out. They must not have expected the rest of us to show in time."

"What do you mean? Who were those kids, anyway? Where'd they get so strong?"

"The questions are going to have to wait," said Rainmaker. The papers that had been scattered in Kat's fall started to swirl around the office as Rainmaker descended with Grunge and Freefall on a cushion of wind. "The rest of them could be back any minute. We've got to get out of here."

" 'Rest of them?' There's more?" Kat asked.

"Come on," Rainmaker said, wincing as she handed Kat the shoulder bag that she had retrieved from the office above.

"And what happened to you?"

"Later," Sarah replied. "We'll fill you in after we get somewhere safe."

Sarah took her arm, and started to lead Kat toward the exit. Kat craned her head around to stare up through the hole at the Girlsworld.com office with helpless longing. "But . . . but . . . ," she pleaded.

She didn't bother finishing the sentence, though. She recognized that her friends knew more about the situation than she did. And she knew they were right.

Kat's heart sank with the realization. The opportunity had seemed so perfect for her. She wanted it so badly. But it looked like a normal life just wasn't in the cards for her right now.

Or maybe ever.

CHAPTER 10

Manhattan's East Village was one of the city's more eclectic neighborhoods. For decades, the area did not have a name of its own, and was simply considered part of the Lower East Side, a slum neighborhood that was home to a true melting pot of Asians, Latinos, Jews, Italians, and any other immigrant group that couldn't afford better living conditions elsewhere. However, as space grew scarce in the neighboring, bohemian neighborhood of Greenwich Village, spiky-haired hipsters with multiple piercings began to spill over in search of more affordable rents. The irony, of course, was that, over time, the increased interest in the East Village led to gentrification and bargains becoming as scarce as in Greenwich Village proper.

Still, thanks to rent control laws that kept the cost of living reasonably affordable for long-time residents, the rising rents didn't drive out the older generation completely. The result was that the neighborhood had become a quirky blend where white-haired old-timers walked the streets side-by-side with teens and twentysomethings sporting leather outfits and dyed purple hair.

In the heart of the East Village was the Hometown Tavern, a small, dingy bar that was located just below street level in one of the apartment buildings on Saint Mark's Place. Sandwiched among used record stores and alternative fashion salons, the smoky bar was clearly intended to cater to an older crowd. In contrast to the strobe lighting and molded plastic that characterized the surrounding establishments, the Hometown looked like nothing more or less than a typical low-end neighborhood bar, with a few simple wooden tables, a dart board, and a jukebox whose selections ran the gamut from big band oldies to more recent hip hop hits.

Bobby glanced casually around the room. "Not exactly our usual kind of hangout."

"That's pretty much the point," Sarah muttered. "These kids know way too much about us. We can't risk going to any of the places where we usually hang."

Grunge fingered his glass with distaste. "Or risk ordering a brew? C'mon, we've gotta be able to do better'n ginger ale."

Sarah rolled her eyes. "Sorry. I didn't think to grab your fake ID from the apartment when we were running for our lives."

Gen[13] huddled around a table in the back of the Hometown Tavern, looking deflated. The day hadn't been one of the team's greatest triumphs . . . and it showed. Thanks to a quick stop at a nearby drug store, Kat had been able to help Sarah tape up her damaged ribs in the ladies' room, and some aspirin helped to dull the pain a bit. Still, Sarah was hurting. In fact, everyone was hurting, to some degree, from the injuries they'd sustained in their battles with Gen[14]. No one looked comfortable in the hard, wooden chairs that the bar had provided, and all of them wore facial expressions that showed just how demoralized they felt. None of them had been given the chance to take a shower or tend to their bumps and bruises. Only Kat had changed her clothes, replacing her shredded suit with an "I ♥ NY" t-shirt and a pair of biker shorts that she had bought from a sidewalk vendor and put on in the Ladies' room at the bar. It wasn't a look that would win her any fashion awards, but it would draw less attention than the tattered remains of an outfit that looked like it had been through a war.

"So, what now?" Bobby asked. "We just try to stay

out of sight? We never go back home, or to anyplace we've set foot in before?"

"Not never," said Kat. "Just until we get this thing settled."

"Yeah, but how long's that going to be?" Bobby heaved a disgusted sigh. "Same old, same old."

"What's that supposed to mean?"

"What it sounds like. After all that time on the run, we finally get to stop hiding from I.O. We get a nice place, a little downtime. And then, just when we're starting to chill . . . Boom! Here we are, right back in the same kind of place all over again. This gig is getting old."

"I can't believe we got whipped by a bunch of kids," Grunge mumbled.

"This is *not* the same place all over again," Sarah said to Bobby. "This isn't like running from I.O. Things are different now . . ."

"Yeah?" said Bobby. "Like how?"

"Like we're older now. We're more experienced than we were when we started out. And this time, at least, we're not stuck fighting someone with the resources of the whole U.S. Government."

"Really? How do you know?" Bobby challenged. "We don't know where those kids came from. Maybe we *are* fighting the whole U.S. Government.

"All I know is that here we are again, back on the run. Adios, New York. Next stop, Montana!"

"Look," said Kat. "Nobody's going to Montana. We are not running away. But we've got to face facts. Those kids outnumber us. They're much more powerful than we are. They're well-organized. And so far, they haven't shown any hesitation about hurting us or anyone who gets in their way."

"Plus," Sarah added, counting off her points on her fingers, "they know who we are. They know where we live. They know so much about us that they already planned out who was going to fight whom before they showed up."

Kat picked up the line of reasoning. "And we know zip about them. That gives the other side a significant advantage. We can't afford to ignore it."

Bobby thought that over for a bit. What they were saying made sense. He shrugged and let his attitude drop away. "Yeah, I know. You're right. My bad. I was just . . ."

"You're upset, you're exhausted, and you're not looking forward to any of this," Kat said, nodding. "I understand. We all feel that way. This thing's taken a lot out of all of us." She reached out and laid a hand on Roxy's arm. Roxy flinched away.

Roxy wasn't ready for physical contact with Kat just yet. Now that some time had passed, Roxy realized that everything she had seen was just a hallucination. Hallucination or not, though, it had hit too close to home. Her head told her that the people around her were her friends and that they loved her. But it was going to take a while for her head to get back in charge.

Even though Roxy wasn't about to say any of that out loud, it was obvious to everyone that, whatever Roxy had gone through, the trauma had left its mark. Roxy was still unusually quiet. She still sat with her arms wrapped around herself for security. Her color still wasn't quite back to normal. And her eyes still carried a slightly haunted look.

They were concerned about her, but there was only so much they could do about it. Until she was ready to open up, they couldn't address whatever was bothering her directly. In the meantime, all they could offer was quiet support.

"So what do we do next?" Bobby asked.

Kat straightened up in her chair as she stepped into the leadership role with an easy confidence. It wasn't difficult to see why Lynch had named Kat as the field leader of Gen[13] without any real protest from any of the others. "Well, eventually, we're going to have to find a place to stay for the night," she said. "Out of all of us, I've probably got the most cash on me, but even that's starting to run low. We'll have to decide whether we want to risk using a credit card or ATM. If they're tapped into the computer networks, that could give our position away.

"In the meantime, though, I suppose the easiest thing would be to try to close the information gap a little. Let's begin by putting together whatever we do know about these guys."

Kat reached down and pulled a pen out of her shoulder bag. She grabbed a couple of bar napkins from the center of the table and prepared to write. "All right, what do we know?"

"They whipped us good," said Grunge.

"Besides that."

"They got this weird Stepford Kids thing going on. All, like, zombiefied or something," said Grunge. "No emotions."

"Could they be robots? Androids?" Sarah offered.

Bobby shook his head. "I don't think so. I got *real* up close and personal with one of them." He suppressed a shudder at the memory of Growing Boy in his mouth. "He didn't feel metal or synthetic or anything. He felt like flesh and blood to me."

Kat wrote on the napkin:
NO EMOTIONS—HUMAN?

"Okay," she said, "that's a start. What else?"

"They call themselves Gen¹⁴," said Bobby.

"Good. That implies a couple of things right there."

"Assuming they didn't just take the name because they thought it sounded cool," Bobby replied. "But it could mean they're gen-actives."

"From the generation after us," Sarah added. "Like Roxy said before, you'd think it would mean they're our kids."

"Whoa!" Grunge said again. "Don't look at me!"

Sarah smiled indulgently. "Relax, stud-boy. They're too old. You would've had to be an incredibly precocious five-year-old."

Grunge looked miffed. "Yeah? You saying I wasn't?"

"Still," Kat said, chewing thoughtfully on the top of her pen, "something like that would fit with their being so much stronger than we are. Y'know, like we're more powerful than our parents from Gen^{12}."

"Don't tell me you buy the Li'l Grunge and His Horny Pals 'n' Gals' theory . . . ?" Sarah said, with a skeptical look.

"No, of course not," Kat replied. "But we've seen stranger things than these kids turning out to be ours. Theoretically, there are ways it could work."

Bobby pointed at her, getting it. "Time travel!"

"Theoretically."

Sarah was unconvinced. "Isn't that just a little too *Twilight Zone*?"

"What isn't, these days?" Kat replied.

"It would explain why they know so much about us . . . ," Bobby said, mulling it over.

Kat looked to Sarah for confirmation, which came in the form of a half-hearted shrug. Kat wrote on the napkin: *Gen^{14}—OUR KIDS? TIME TRAVEL?*

"There's a much simpler answer, though," Sarah said.

"What's that?" Kat asked.

"I.O. They know a lot about us. They're the ones who activated our powers. Why not these kids', too?"

"For one thing, there is no I.O. anymore," Grunge said. "I.O. bit the big one, remember?"

"Sure," Sarah replied, "but who knows when the kids were created? Besides, we know there's old I.O. weaponry floating around on the black market. Who's to say whether some of their other tech might be out there, too?"

"It's possible, but that's not the kind of equipment most people off the street would be able to operate," Kat said. "With a gun, no matter how sophisticated it is, you basically just point it and pull the trigger. The kind of equipment that activated our gen-factors is way trickier. You'd need the knowledge to make it work, too." Still, she added *I.O. TECH?* to the napkin anyway. No point to ruling out possibilities just yet.

"All right," Kat said. "I don't think we'll be able to nail down too much more about their origins yet, but at least we've got some ideas to think about. Let's turn to the more practical side now. How many of them are there?"

Bobby fingered his goatee thoughtfully as he searched his memory. "I dunno . . . Maybe, like, ten?"

"Sounds right," Sarah agreed. "Unless there are more that we haven't met yet."

"Always the optimist," Bobby said with a smirk.

"It's a good point," Kat said. "For now, I guess we'll just stick with the ones we know about. Who are they? What can they do?"

"Growing Boy," said Burnout. "Shrinks down tiny and grows to giant size. Sometimes in the most inconvenient places."

"I can think of a more inconvenient place, dude," said Grunge with a grin.

"Up yours."

Grunge threw up his arms. "*Ding ding ding!* That's right! Would you like to quit now or go for the million dollars?"

Kat wrote down the information on Growing Boy and smiled to herself. At least her teammates were starting to act more like themselves again. Being proactive was working wonders.

"And Riptide," Burnout added. "Turns into a jet of water."

"Strong?" Kat asked.

"Oh, yeah," Burnout replied.

"There's Reverb," Sarah added. "At first, I thought he hit me with telekinesis, but from his code name, it was probably some kind of sonic blast."

Kat nodded. "You mean that boy with the curly hair? I'll go along with that. My ears are still ringing from whatever he did inside my head."

"So he can control it," Sarah said. "Big, explosive blasts, like with me, or more targeted, pinpoint attacks, like when he hit you."

Kat wrote it down.

"Rave," Sarah said with a shiver. "She scrambles your senses, so you can't even tell which way is up."

"For free? Cool . . . ," said Grunge, with a wistful smile.

"Oh, really? Then I'll let you fight her next time."

Sarah turned back to Kat and placed a finger on the napkin. "Add in Sidestep. She's a teleporter. She can send parts of her body to other places. She's also the one who helped Reverb escape after they blew the attack on you."

"She probably handles transport for Gen[14] in general," Kat said as she wrote.

"That'd make sense."

"My turn!" said Grunge. "Okay. There's Slash. Dude turns his arms into blades. No big deal. But Override can take over your bod, which is really whacked. And Knock-out's all, like, superchick. She's gotta be as strong as Kat."

"Stronger," Kat said, still writing. She completed her notes and looked up. "Any others?"

"There's that blonde girl. The leader," Burnout said. "I didn't catch her name, though."

"Anybody get it?"

There was a brief pause. Then, looking down, Roxy mumbled something.

Kat turned gently toward her sister. "I'm sorry, Roxy," she said in a kindly tone. "I didn't hear. What did you say?"

"Highwire. Her name's Highwire."

"Great. What does she do?"

"She's an acrobat," Roxy said quietly. "She's also . . ." Roxy paused, remembering the reaction she'd received in her hallucination. "She's . . . really fast."

Roxy braced herself for the ridicule, but this time, there wasn't any.

"Okay, thanks," Kat said. She added *HIGHWIRE: Acrobat—agility, speed* to the napkin. "Are there any others you want to add?"

Roxy didn't say anything for what seemed like a very long time. All eyes watched her with concern, until she said, in a very small voice, ". . . Bogeyman."

Kat nodded slowly. Judging from Roxy's reaction, Kat assumed that Bogeyman must be the one who'd affected her so badly. Kat couldn't imagine what he'd done to her. Softly, she asked, "And what's his power?"

Again, there was a pause. Roxy glanced at her friends, then back down at the floor. "I . . ." She held herself a little more tightly. ". . . I don't want to talk about it."

The others exchanged worried glances. Grunge's jaw set and his eyes narrowed in anger.

Kat stretched out her hand to stroke Roxy's arm. "I understand," Kat said. "It's okay."

She started to move on to address the others, but stopped herself. "Listen," Kat told Roxy, "I know you know this, but I'm going to say it anyway. We're your friends, Roxy. I'm your sister. We love you. You can do anything, you can tell us anything, and nothing's ever going to change that.

"Nobody's going to make you talk about anything that you don't want to talk about. But you need to understand that whatever that kid did back there, that's on him. It doesn't affect how we feel about you.

"If you can bring yourself to tell us about him, it'll help us prepare. That way, hopefully, he won't be able to do it to anyone else next time. But if it's too much for you to talk about right now, that's fine. No one'll hold it against you. It's totally your call."

"No pressure," Bobby agreed.

"Whatever you want," said Sarah.

Grunge draped a brawny arm around Roxy's shoulders and gave her a squeeze.

Roxy was quiet for a long time. She chewed on her

lip, her brow furrowed, as she faced the memories. Then, finally, she spoke.

"He . . . showed me things," she said.

"What kind of things?" Kat asked quietly.

"Scary things."

"You mean, he cast illusions?"

Roxy nodded.

"But you didn't know they were illusions."

Roxy shook her head.

Kat continued to stroke Roxy's arm. Her sister seemed on the verge of tears. Kat didn't know what Bogeyman could have shown Roxy to scare her so badly, but she decided against prying further. Roxy would tell her at some point, if she felt the need. To affect her this deeply, though, it obviously had to have struck a nerve. Kat suspected that Bogeyman had preyed upon some deep-seated fear that had already been lurking in Roxy's psyche. Roxy wasn't the type to fall apart like this otherwise.

She didn't say any of that to Roxy, though.

"That's really helpful," said Kat. "And it was brave of you to share it. I know it wasn't easy. Thanks."

Kat lifted her pen, wrote *BOGEYMAN: Fear-based illusions*, and took a deep breath.

She then proceeded to run her pen lightly down the list, and looked around at the group. "Okay, that's ten. Are we missing any? Is that all of them?"

There was a chorus of shrugs and tentative nods.

"Good. All right, we've got a list of the bad guys, and a list of their strengths. Now, how about weaknesses? Anybody spot any weaknesses?"

The others shifted uncomfortably in the silence. The jukebox continued to play. No one spoke up.

"Hmm. Yeah, me either," said Kat.

Bobby shrugged. "They're short . . . ," he offered.

"Well, never mind. Let's put our heads together," Kat said. "Maybe we can figure out some strategy."

"Strategy? Oh, man," Grunge said. "Geez, where's Mister L when you need . . . ?"

Grunge's voice trailed off as his eyes grew wide—and so did everyone else's. They sat there for a moment, stunned. Then, as one, they all said the same word:

"Lynch!"

Everyone started talking at once.

"Where's . . . ?"

"How'd we forget . . . ?"

"What if he went back . . . ?"

"Could he be a target . . . ?"

Bobby got up with a grim look on his face. "I'm going to call his cell."

He walked to the back of the bar and dropped a quarter in the pay telephone that hung on the wall. He waited, tapping his foot impatiently, as the phone rang once.

Twice.

Halfway through the third ring, someone picked up on the other end.

"Dad?" Bobby asked anxiously.

"Robert Lane?" said the voice on the other end.

Bobby's eyes widened in shock. Whoever it was, it wasn't Lynch. The voice was younger and higher in pitch. It was calm to the point of being almost monotone.

"Who is this?!" Bobby demanded.

"Mister Lynch meddled in affairs that he should have left alone."

"If you've hurt him . . ."

"There is no need for empty threats. Mister Lynch has, perhaps, seen better days, but I assure you that he is still among the living."

"You assure me . . . ?! Put him on the phone!"

"To allow him the opportunity to pass on a cleverly coded message? No."

"Then how do I know he's alive?"

"We could send you a finger. A pathologist could tell you that it came from a living person. Would that be sufficient?"

"Now, you listen up," Bobby hissed. "I am going to

give you *one* chance to let my father go! After that, I'm going to—"

"No. *You* have only one chance to secure his release. Listen carefully."

Bobby listened. Two minutes later, he slammed the receiver back into its cradle and stormed back toward the table.

"Uh oh. That doesn't look good," said Sarah.

Bobby came to a stop in front of his friends. He didn't sit. The muscles in his face were taut with tension. "They've got him."

"Ohmigosh," said Kat.

"But he's not the one they want. The kid on the phone said they were willing to make a trade. My dad . . ."

". . . for the five of us," Kat said.

"You got it."

"It's a trick," said Sarah.

"Dude," Grunge said quietly, "you gotta know they're not gonna let him walk outta there."

"Doesn't matter," said Bobby. "I spent most of my life without a father. I'm not going to lose him again now.

"The trade's happening in one hour. I'm going. You guys can decide for yourselves."

The rest of the team looked at each other.

Kat was the first to break the silence. "If it wasn't for Mister Lynch and his training, we'd have been dead a long time ago," she said. "I'm going."

"Count me in," said Sarah.

"I'm down," said Grunge.

They watched Roxy with sympathetic, tentative expressions. None of them could be certain about what her answer would be.

Roxy raised her head. Her face was pale, her eyes bloodshot from tears. But her jaw was set, and a determined fire burned in her eyes.

"Let's get 'em," Roxy said.

CHAPTER 11

Night had fallen by the time a yellow taxicab pulled up to a curb on West Fourteeth Street. The air was cold and crisp, although the snow from the night before had begun to melt, dissolving into dirty, brown goop.

The Gen[13] crew clambered out of the cab. They stood on the curb and waited as Kat paid the fare.

"I'm sorry," Kat said to the driver. "I'd give you a tip, but this is the last of my cash."

"Yeah, right," the driver replied. "Lousy club kids."

The driver pulled away in a sweeping U-turn that sprayed them with the dirty slush.

"I hate this city!" Sarah said, trying in vain to clean the slush from her clothes.

The far west end of West Fourteeth Street, down near the river, was taken up primarily by wholesale butchers and meat markets. There was nothing fancy about these buildings, which were designed for function over form. Many of them seemed to consist of little more than loading docks, with slanted metal awnings above them to protect the workers from the elements when they had to load the meat onto trucks in bad weather. The long tractor trailers parked outside the loading docks stood in mute testament to the thousands upon thousands of pounds of meat that these suppliers sold to restaurants, hotels, and retail stores on a daily basis.

The day typically began early here. Some high-end chefs preferred to select and buy their own ingredients fresh, before preparing morning meals. As a result, the suppliers had to be ready equally early, and open for business.

The flip side to the early openings was that these businesses tended not to stay open too late at night. Apart from an occasional car heading down toward the West Side Highway, the street was deserted. There was none of the neon and bright lights that could be found in so much of the city. The only substantial illumination lay in equally-spaced pools of light that were thrown by the streetlamps overhead to break up the heavy shadows.

"Good place for an ambush," Sarah whispered

"Stay sharp, everyone," Kat said in an undertone. "They could be anywhere."

"Literally," Bobby replied. "One of them's a teleporter, remember? For all we know, they could be on the French Riviera right now."

"Hold up, amigos. Time for a little protective action." Grunge took a moment to absorb the molecular structure of one of the cobblestones that still stuck up through the asphalt in patches here. He started to hum the theme song from *Rocky* as his skin darkened, turned gray and grainy, and then stopped being skin at all. In the blink of an eye, Grunge's body had morphed into solid rock. Grunge thrust out a finger in an exaggerated wrestling pose. *"Can you smell what the Rock is cooking?!"*

"Yeah, from all the way over here," Sarah whispered. "Keep it down."

"Oh, for. . . . Will you guys please shut up?" Roxy snapped. "There's a fight coming, y'know?" She produced a disposable lighter and lit the cigarette between her lips, without taking her eyes off her shadowy surroundings.

Kat looked at Roxy with concern. Roxy had started to get past her fear, which was a good thing. But, as near as Kat could tell, she was overcoming it by channeling the anxiety into attitude instead. It was a tactic that Kat had seen Roxy use before. In fact, she suspected that Roxy had been using it all her life. By and large, it had always seemed to work reasonably well for her. But Roxy was

145

really scared now, so the strategy had wound up taking her beyond attitude and all the way into a raging, free-floating anger. Kat worried that it could make her careless.

Actually, Kat had similar concerns about Bobby, as well. Bobby was worried about his father. He was furious with his captors. He was just too emotionally involved.

Ordinarily, Kat would have trusted either of them with her life. In fact, she'd done it many times, without question or a moment's hesitation. But even by their standards, they were up against an unusually dangerous foe this time. Every one of them needed to be calm and clearheaded. They couldn't afford to get sloppy.

Ironically, it was Kat's preoccupation with such issues that almost kept her from noticing the thirty-foot-long tractor-trailer that was hurtling through the air toward them.

Kat braced herself to try to catch the airborne vehicle, although she knew full well that it was too big to stop completely. Even if she could absorb the truck's forward momentum, its sheer size meant that it would probably wrap itself around her and still do a whole lot of damage to the rest of the team.

Before it could come to that, though, Roxy hit the oncoming truck with a massive burst of negative gravity. Still in motion, the truck veered sharply upward in mid-air to soar over their heads.

It would have been a good idea . . . except that it sent the truck smashing straight through the second-story wall of the meat packing plant behind them. Broken bricks and mortar rained down from the wall. Instead of keeping an eye out for Gen[14], the team had to devote their full attention to intercepting the shower of bricks with flame, wind, weightlessness, and fists before it could smash down on the heroes.

Not to mention dealing with the falling truck.

It was the sort of mistake that never would have happened if Roxy hadn't been distracted by her anger. It was exactly the kind of thing Kat had been worried about. And it kept the team occupied long enough for Gen[14] to be all over them.

It was as though Gen[14] had appeared from nowhere. In fact, with Sidestep around, they probably had.

The well-coordinated attack skipped the preliminaries and sailed straight into high gear. With both numbers and power on their side, Gen[14] had the advantage. And as they launched into their offensive, it was clear that they not only knew it, but had no intention of giving it up. Within seconds, the battle was raging on five fronts simultaneously.

Knockout laid into Grunge with a flurry of titanic blows. Unlike their last fight, Grunge wasn't stuck as a motionless bronze statue anymore. This time, he could move freely, and he had the might of a two-hundred-pound boulder on his side.

On the other hand, though, Knockout's strength could shatter boulders.

Grunge managed to get in a few good shots of his own, but his rocky form was starting to crack under Knockout's pounding. His only hope was to keep parrying and deflecting the rapid-fire series of punches.

Because a solid one could take his head off.

It took all of Grunge's concentration to keep up. He couldn't do so much as spout a wisecrack. Then, Knockout did something that took him completely by surprise: She dropped to the ground.

A split-second later, Grunge knew why. With Knockout out of the way, Reverb hit Grunge with a tightly focused blast. Knockout's assault had already compromised the integrity of Grunge's body, leaving a weblike network of cracks behind. Reverb's vibrations threatened to finish the job.

He was literally going to shake Grunge to pieces.

For her part, Freefall had eyes for only one member of Gen[14]. As soon as she caught a glimpse of Bogeyman, she streaked toward him like an avenging bolt of lightning.

Freefall rocketed through the air, with her body arched forward to strike and her face twisted in a grimace of hate. Only one thought filled her brain:

You're mine, *you little piece of—*

If Freefall had been using any caution at all, she probably would have spotted the shimmering patch of air in front of her. But she was in no state to notice much of anything at the moment. Freefall sailed through Sidestep's teleportational portal at top speed . . .

. . . and reappeared scant inches from a solid brick wall. Freefall was still going at top speed, but not for long.

Freefall hit the wall with a sickening thud. Barely conscious, she fell to the ground below in a heap.

Growing Boy was already waiting there. The twenty-foot 'tween towered over Freefall's crumpled form. Of all the members of Gen[14], Growing Boy had fared the worst in the previous battles, and he wasn't looking too bad. Growing Boy wore a few bandages to cover the burns from his previous fight with Burnout, but they didn't seem to be holding him back at all.

The streetlights cast a shadow over Freefall as Growing Boy raised a foot that was half the length of her entire body. Then, he brought it down.

When Rainmaker dove out of the way of the falling truck, she hit the ground rolling. The maneuver sent waves of blinding pain through Rainmaker's injured side, but it was better than staying where she was and waiting for the truck. Ordinarily, she would have cushioned the impact of hitting the ground with a series of forward tumbles that carried her out of danger, then used the momentum to bring herself back up onto her feet. This time, though, the pain from her ribs broke her concentration. Her arm buckled, sending her awkwardly to the ground.

Rainmaker forced herself to her feet, to find Slash waiting there to meet her. With a grunt, he swung one of his razor-sharp arms toward her throat. If he had connected, it would have severed her head. But Rainmaker dropped back down to the ground in time for his blade to cut nothing more than a few locks of her long, black hair.

In a single, fluid motion, Rainmaker landed on her palms and countered with a sweeping, roundhouse kick that knocked Slash's feet out from under him. She jumped back up to her feet as he hit the pavement.

Slash quickly rose to a crouch. Rainmaker was already extending her palms toward him. "Back off, Switchblade Boy, or I'll rust you solid!"

Without a word, Slash used his legs to launch himself up toward her. His arms were extended straight out like a pair of sabers.

The metal blades were perfect conductors. Rainmaker called up a bolt of lightning that sent Slash flying back where he came from. Slash skidded across the ground, already unconscious.

Rainmaker brushed the dust off her clothes. "That's that. One down."

She turned away from Slash, and came face to face with another of the Gen^{14} kids.

Their eyes locked.

Sarah froze in place.

"Who are you guys? Why are you doing all this?"

Even as they battled, Fairchild kept trying to get answers out of Highwire. Highwire wasn't going for it, though.

Great. Just great, Fairchild thought. *Just when I need information, I finally find a villain who* doesn't *like to gloat while she fights.*

On paper, a fight between the two team leaders would have looked like a total mismatch—Mike Tyson versus Woody Allen. Fairchild had almost every advantage over Highwire. Fairchild was bigger. She was virtually invulnerable. And she was a whole lot stronger.

But Highwire was a whole lot faster.

Like Roxy before her, Fairchild soon found that, no matter how hard she tried, she just couldn't land a blow.

Highwire was in constant motion, always flipping or tumbling just in time to throw Fairchild off-balance or stay just out of reach.

Conversely, there didn't seem to be much that Highwire could do to Fairchild, either. Fairchild was so much stronger that Highwire's own attacks just glanced off her. She hadn't even managed to trip Fairchild or knock her over. The fight was rapidly turning into a stalemate.

Which puzzled Kat. From everything she'd seen and heard about before this, it was obvious that Gen¹⁴'s attacks were meticulously planned. Each of them was assigned to a target that he or she was uniquely equipped to deal with. Choosing to send Highwire after her just didn't make sense. Why wouldn't they . . .

Ohhhh, Kat thought.

Fairchild dropped her hands and stood still. "You can stop now," she said.

Highwire landed in a crouch and eyed Fairchild suspiciously. She leaped up and flipped head over heels to kick Fairchild in the jaw. Not only did Fairchild hold her ground, but her head barely moved with the impact.

"You're not supposed to beat me, are you?" Fairchild asked. "You're supposed to distract me while someone else gets into position. So who am I *really* going to be fighting?"

Suddenly, Fairchild grabbed her head, reeling, as Rave made Fairchild's senses explode in psychedelic anarchy.

"Oh, not again," Burnout said. He glided up in a sweeping loop around Riptide's cascading jet of water. "This whole fire-water thing's getting way old. Let's just cut to the chase for a change:

"Where's my father?"

Burnout pulled back to give himself a little distance and punctuated his question with a small burst of flame. There was a sizzling sound as the fire hit the column of water and boiled part of it away into steam. But Riptide didn't answer. Instead, the towering water spout curved up and over to circle around and rush toward Burnout with the strength and power of a runaway train.

Burnout had absolutely no patience left for this nonsense. While they were dancing around this way, his father could be dying. Every second counted, and he had no intention of wasting even one more on this loser.

Reaching deep down inside himself, Burnout conjured up a superheated mass of intense flame—enough to vaporize Riptide in an eyeblink. Burnout didn't know whether Riptide would ever be able to reconstitute himself after the blast hit. But as he let it fly, he didn't much care.

Suddenly, the water parted. The spout began to split into two parallel streams, keeping pace with Burnout's attack. The ball of fiery plasma shot straight down the middle, staying true to its course without touching either of the streams surrounding it.

As the water divided, though, it gave Burnout a view of what stood behind the torrent. He reacted with horror when he saw the new target that was now directly in the path of the blazing assault.

It was Lynch.

Lynch *was* there! He'd been running toward them, probably planning to help. But Lynch froze in his tracks when the water split and he saw the speeding mass of flames. It was heading straight for him, and it was too close to dodge.

Bobby shot forward to try to stop the runaway missile. Lynch tried to jump out of the way.

They were both too late.

The white-hot ball of plasma hit Lynch full on. He erupted into flame.

"*Nnnnoooooooo!*" Bobby screamed.

It was hard even to see Lynch through the inferno now. He screamed in agony as his body jerked around in a macabre dance before dropping to the ground.

Bobby tried everything he could to extinguish the blaze. He tried to beat out the flames. He tried to absorb them into his body. But by the time the fire was out,

Lynch was little more than a blackened cinder. Every inch of his body was covered with third-degree burns.

Bobby was numb with shock. He cradled Lynch in his arms. Bits of Lynch's skin flaked off into ash at his touch.

"Dad! Dad!" Bobby cried. "Talk to me! Say something!"

Lynch coughed, and even that simple reflex made him convulse in pain. Through his tears, Bobby could see that every movement increased Lynch's suffering all the more. Slowly, painfully, Lynch opened his eyes. He moved his lips feebly, trying to speak.

"It's okay, Dad. It's okay," said his anguished son. "I'm here. I'm listening. It's okay."

Lynch's face registered the unimaginable agony that grew as he tried to form words. But he had never let pain stop him before. He had something to tell his son, and nothing was going to prevent it. Bobby could see the herculean effort that it took.

When Lynch's voice finally came, it was a harsh, raspy whisper. "B . . . Bobby . . ."

"Yes, Dad. I'm here."

"Yo . . . you . . ."

Bobby leaned in closer to hear the muted words.

"You . . . you . . . killed me."

Lynch died.

Bobby's scream tore through the night.

Standing over him, Bogeyman reacted with no visible emotion whatsoever. The illusion was so perfect that Bobby didn't even notice when Riptide started to drown him.

As Reverb's vibrations intensified, it took everything Grunge had to try and hold himself together. Already, the cracks were widening. Chips of rock were flying from his body. It wouldn't be long before he shattered completely.

If Grunge kept this form, he was doomed. But if he changed back to normal, the deep cracks would become gaping wounds. He'd bleed to death in seconds. Either way, he was finished.

Grunge had to do something. He stamped his foot down in a mound of slush . . .

. . . and started to change.

Instantly, his body began to soften. Its color shifted to a murky brown. Instead of chiseled and hard, Grunge became watery and semi-solid.

The vibrations ripped Grunge's body into a million pieces. Bits of Grunge splattered all over everyone and everything in sight.

Reverb and Knockout stood there for a bit, gazing impassively at the mess that had been Grunge as they checked their kill. Satisfied, they nodded to each other and headed off to make sure the rest of Gen[13] was under control.

. . . And the pieces started to move.

Little by little, the bits of slush oozed, flowed, and trickled back toward the spot where Grunge's feet had been. Slowly at first, but then more quickly, the mound grew until it resembled a filthy, brownish snowman.

A filthy, brownish snowman that looked a lot like Grunge.

The snow-Grunge pumped his dripping fists in the air. He threw back his head and shouted: "Who da man!"

Grunge's desperate, last-ditch plan had worked! He knew that if he let himself be blown apart in his rocky form, all of the bits would have to be pieced together perfectly before he could have a prayer of returning to human form. And that wasn't likely to happen in his lifetime.

But water and slush don't work that way. They flow and mix. Grunge had prayed that merely getting the bits back in contact with each other would be enough to let him reshape himself. From all appearances, it looked like he was right.

Snow-Grunge looked up to see Rainmaker hovering

just above him. "Yo, Sarah!" he called. "Let's go kick some underage butt!"

Rainmaker gestured. Instantly, a howling storm appeared from nowhere, pelting Grunge with a heavy downpour of driving rain. "Sarah, no! Stop!" he cried. "When the water hits me . . ."

But it was too late. Grunge was already melting. The rain was literally washing him away.

The strategy that had saved Grunge's life was working against him now. He'd managed to re-form his body because the nature of the watery slush was to flow together and blend. However, if this new water mixed in with the water molecules in his body, Grunge wasn't sure that he'd be able to separate himself back out. Ever.

Rainmaker watched the scene without any visible sign of emotion. On the outside, anyway. Deep in the recesses of her mind, Sarah was screaming. Ever since Override had taken control of her body, that was all she could do.

Grunge struggled mightily to hold his body together. At the same time, he was also fighting to revert to flesh and blood before he reached the point of no return. Slowly, painfully, Grunge regained his human form—

—just in time for a hurricane-force wind to blow him off his feet. He tumbled helplessly through the air, smashing into the side of a commercial van that was parked at the side of the road. The side of the van crumpled under the impact. Grunge fell onto the street, unconscious.

Rainmaker's stolen body looked around to see how the rest of the battle was progressing. Burnout had already passed out from lack of oxygen by the time Riptide dropped him on the ground. Freefall was still sprawled motionless across the sidewalk where Growing Boy had left her.

Only Fairchild was still on her feet, reeling under Rave's sensory assault. Rainmaker called down an immense bolt of lightning that lit up the sky for miles around. The bolt struck Fairchild with an electrical blast that could be measured only in megavolts.

VERSION 2.0

Still under the effects of Rave's powers, Fairchild never felt a thing. But that didn't prevent her body from suffering the effects. She went rigid, and her red hair stood on end. The air smelled of smoke as Fairchild lit up like a lightbulb, then went dark and collapsed. Her breathing was shallow as she lay there in the gutter. But at least she was breathing.

Rainmaker and Highwire exchanged a nod. There was just one last piece of unfinished business to wrap up.

Rainmaker summoned up one last bolt of lightning.

This one was aimed at herself.

CHAPTER 12

Slowly, Roxy opened her eyes and brought them into focus.

"Hey, babe," said Grunge. "You feeling okay?"

Roxy thought she was okay, but she was still struggling to get coherent thoughts to gel. As she drifted, little by little, back into consciousness, the numbness was replaced by a soreness and a dull ache that crept over her whole body.

Why did she hurt so much?

She fought through the cloud of cotton balls that filled her head and searched her memory. The last thing she could remember was . . .

Was . . .

Oh, right. Flying headfirst into a brick wall.

Yeah, that would do it, she thought. Fortunately, Roxy had managed to cut down Growing Boy's weight just before he stomped her flat. Otherwise, she knew, she'd be hurting a lot worse—if at all.

Roxy needed a cigarette.

"Who, me? I'm just spiffy," she told Grunge, her voice dripping with sarcasm.

Grunge paused for a moment. He listened to her words, then her tone, and his eyes lit up. "Hey!" he exclaimed. "*That's* my sweetie! You're back!"

It took Roxy a minute to figure out what he meant. But then she got it. Despite Roxy's physical pains, time and a taste of oblivion had left her in better mental shape than she'd been in all night. Thanks to her earlier fit of blind rage, she was pretty much past the helpless terror that came with Bogeyman's attack. As long as she didn't think about it (or so she realized, quickly pushing the thoughts away), all that was left was a tinge of anxiety floating around the edges of her psyche. Meanwhile, the bout of unconsciousness had mostly dissipated the rage itself—helped along, of course, by the memory of how stupidly she'd acted.

Roxy still felt a bit peeved, but she'd get over it. Besides, all things considered, she figured she was entitled.

Now that she was more fully awake, Roxy looked around at her surroundings. She was relieved to see that the rest of her friends were there, too. Most of them had awakened before her. Only Sarah's eyes were still closed. Roxy could see that Sarah was breathing quietly, though, so it wasn't as bad as it could have been.

Then, Roxy did a double-take as her mind registered the older, black-clad figure beside Grunge.

"Mister L!" Roxy cried. "You're alive!"

It was indeed their mentor. There were manacles around his wrists and ankles. His numerous cuts and bruises indicated that he'd been through a phenomenal beating. But he was alive.

"Funny, that's what we all said, too," Bobby remarked.

"Nice to know you all care," Lynch said, deadpan, as his eyes studied the edges of the room.

That was the good news.

The bad news was that, while it was true that they were all together, they were all together in a small, dirty cell with concrete walls and a reinforced steel door that didn't have so much as a keyhole, let alone a knob or window. The floor of the cell couldn't have measured more than about eight feet by eight feet, hardly enough room for six people. And that was assuming you could even see the floor through the thick layer of dust that covered it like a shroud.

The only things that weren't covered with dust were their shackles. The manacles circled each of their wrists and ankles, and gleamed under the fluorescent lights. A short length of thick chain connected each manacle to the wall, leaving each prisoner suspended a couple of feet above the floor. No wonder Roxy felt like her arms had been through a taffy pull.

They hung in a row that wrapped along two walls of the cell: Roxy on one end, followed by Sarah, Bobby, Grunge, Lynch, and Kat. Dangling there, they looked like someone's twisted idea of a series of family photos. Or maybe a set of animal heads, stuffed and mounted as trophies.

Roxy looked up to see a small video camera that was mounted near the ceiling. It was angled downward, watching them with an unblinking eye.

"Anybody wanna tell me where we are?" Roxy asked.

"Wish we could," Bobby said with a shrug. Or as much of a shrug as he could manage while hanging by his arms.

"And I don't figure anyone's thought of busting out to go take a look?"

"I wish we could do that, too," Kat replied. "Our powers aren't working. It's the restraints."

Roxy took a closer look at the manacles that circled her wrists. Woven through the links of each chain, Roxy noticed, was a cable that led from the cuff into the wall.

Experimentally, Roxy tried to make herself float. But despite her efforts, she only managed to rise an inch or so—not nearly as much as it should have been.

Kat was right. The manacles were some kind of power dampeners. It wasn't the first time that Roxy had encountered the technology. They'd been locked up in these kinds of things before. Back when . . .

Oh.

Suddenly, everything was starting to make sense.

Roxy turned toward the others. "I know who's behind this . . ."

As one, the others all gave a matter-of-fact nod. "Yeah." "Uh-huh." "Yes."

"You too, huh?" she said.

"Yup. Any other questions?" Bobby asked with a wry smile.

"Yeah," Roxy said. "How'd we get in our costumes?"

It was true. Roxy's and Grunge's Gen[13] uniforms weren't all that different from their typical street clothes. For Roxy, it came down to a halter top, mini-skirt, and leather jacket, while the muscular Grunge opted for skin-tight pants with no shirt. However, everyone else had gone through a complete change of wardrobe. Kat's T-shirt and biker shorts had been replaced by a green-and-purple outfit that resembled a French cut bathing suit with long sleeves and boots. Bobby was dressed in a tightly-fitting red top emblazoned with a triangle that pointed down toward his yellow tights. And Sarah, though still unconscious, was now wearing a red-and-turquoise span-dex leotard that left both arms and one leg bare. It was accented by the knee-high, fringed leather boots that she wore as a reminder of her home on the reservation.

The only detail that was missing from any of their uniforms was the metal armbands that Sarah usually wore. In fact, she'd been wearing them before the change of clothes, and Roxy could see them lying on the floor. It was no surprise that their captor had neglected to put them back on Sarah's arms, though. The high-tech bands intensified both the power and the precision of the lightning blasts that Sarah controlled.

The notion that their captor had undressed them and re-dressed them like playthings disturbed Roxy, but it didn't surprise her. If her suspicions about their captor's identity were correct, it wasn't the first time something like this had happened. It was just one more piece of evidence to support her theory.

Sarah started to stir. ". . . Where . . . ?" she mumbled.

Lynch looked at Roxy as he gestured toward Sarah with a tilt of his head. "Your questions should be answered soon. Now that all of us are conscious, I'd expect a personal visit in approximately three . . . two . . . one . . ."

The heavy door slid open.

"Oh, hey, Ivana," said Roxy. "What's up?"

Ivana Baiul stood in the doorway in a mock pout. "Tsk," she said. "No shocked gasps of recognition? No cries of, 'You! It—it can't be you?'

"Weren't you surprised by my little revelation?"

"You're getting predictable, Ivana," said Lynch. "Just like your love of dramatic entrances."

Ivana's choice of clothing didn't particularly make her look like the former head of International Operation's sci-tech division. She was dressed in a clingy, black leather jump suit that showed off her figure to full advantage. Her jet black hair was pulled back in a tight bun. The stiletto heels of her high-top boots added six inches to her height.

However, one glimpse of Ivana's dark eyes and the hard lines of her face would have been enough to convince anyone of the sheer, unflinching ruthlessness that lay not very far beneath Ivana's surface. Ivana had learned long ago that she could use her looks to divert and manipulate the men around her. Even her playful tone was heavy with menace.

Gen^{13} knew what Ivana was like firsthand. When I.O. first brought them together, Ivana had overseen the gauntlet of tests and treatments that was designed to activate the superhuman abilities that came with their gen-factors. As the team struggled to endure the grueling regimen, it quickly became all too clear that Ivana didn't care whether they lived or died. All she cared about was creating her own super-powered, personal army.

Now, apparently, she had.

"Sorry to spoil your surprise," said Kat. "Once we had the chance to think about it, it was pretty obvious. Your fingerprints were all over this thing."

"Who else could crank out gen-active kids?" Bobby said. He chuckled dryly. "And who'd *want* to?"

"How many people would know enough to come after us? Or know enough what each of us can do to pair us up individually against kids who counteract our powers?" Kat added.

"Who else would wait to kill us so she could show off first?" said Roxy. Then, she thought about it for a second. "No, wait—*everyone* we fight does that."

"And who else would fill out that leather S&M suit in all the right—" Grunge looked at Bobby. Now that he wasn't so busy worrying about Roxy, Grunge suddenly remembered their bet. "Um . . . who else would . . . um . . . trash our place?"

Lynch studiously ignored Grunge as he spoke to Ivana. "You even gave your pawns personalities as scintillating as your own."

"Personalities are overrated, Jack. Too much personality in an operative can prove to be more trouble than it's worth," Ivana replied. She gave Gen^{13} an icy glance before looking back at Lynch. "As you well know."

Roxy opened her mouth to lash back with an equally cutting retort, but stopped when Kat caught her eye and shook her head.

"Over time," Ivana continued, "I've found that I prefer my soldiers without a lot of independent thought getting in the way. Simple, slavish obedience is far more satisfying."

Bobby reacted indignantly. "So what, you just lobotomized a bunch of kids?"

"Lobotomized?!" Ivana looked genuinely offended. "Where would be the point in that? Do you honestly believe that I would create a new generation of superpowered operatives, merely to have them wander around aimlessly, drooling oatmeal? Please. I didn't have to lobotomize them. It's far more effective to raise them that way."

"You *raised* them?" Sarah said, surprised. Even though she was still a bit groggy, the notion of a maternal Ivana seemed more than a little ludicrous. It was a little like picturing Lucrezia Borgia at a PTA meeting.

Ivana brought a hand to her lips in false astonishment.

"Oh, my! Don't tell me that, with all my predictable ways, I've actually surprised you!" Her lips curling into a self-satisfied smile, Ivana patted Sarah's cheek. "I've cultivated and reared these children from the finest in fourteenth-generation, gen-active DNA. I hate to be the one to tell you, dear, but you and your Gen[13] friends are outdated. How does it feel to be obsolete?"

" 'Fourteenth-generation . . . ,' " Roxy said. "So they *are* our kids!"

Ivana laughed. "I'm sorry. You must have misheard. I said the *finest* in gen-active DNA. I wouldn't let your gutter-rat genomes anywhere near my prize creations."

"But then, how . . . ?"

Kat nodded, understanding. "We're not the only thirteenth-generation gen-actives."

"Threshold and Bliss," Lynch said.

Threshold and Bliss were the dark shadow of Gen[13]. They'd been abducted by I.O. as children, a full fifteen years before Kat and her friends. All of those years with Ivana and her crew accounted for their much finer control over their powers. Not to mention their sociopathic tendencies, or their utter lack of anything resembling a conscience.

Roxy recoiled with a shudder. *"Ewwww!"* she said. "But—but Threshold is, like, Bliss's brother! Gross!"

"I think she's talking about cell samples and test tubes, Roxy," Kat said.

"So? It's still totally gross!"

"Hey, Sarah!" Grunge exclaimed happily. "You're an aunt!"

Sarah shot him a withering look. It was true. Although she hadn't known it for most of her life, Sarah shared a father with Threshold and Bliss. But it didn't mean that she liked to be reminded of it.

"Even with accelerated aging, it must have taken years to set this up," Lynch said to Ivana. "But I never heard a whisper of it. Craven and the rest of the brass at I.O. had no clue that this operation existed, did they?"

"It's remarkable what one can accomplish with a bit of diverted funding," Ivana replied. "A decommissioned NORAD facility, some 'missing' technology, a small number of hand-picked technicians. . . . Of course, they're all long dead now, the poor dears. It's really quite tragic."

"So even while you were running the Genesis Project to develop Gen^{13} for I.O. . . . ."

". . . they had no idea that I was already a full generation ahead of them."

A silence descended over the room as the implications of Ivana's statement sank in. It wasn't just that Ivana had succeeded in creating her personal army. It wasn't just the thought of what Gen^{14} was capable of doing at Ivana's command. It wasn't even the fact that, with Gen^{13} imprisoned, there was no one who stood a chance of stopping her.

It was that, in all the time they'd opposed Ivana, none of them—including Lynch—had ever suspected that anything like this was going on simultaneously.

Of course, they knew that Ivana always made sure to have an extra ace or two up her sleeve. But the idea that she could have concealed a shadow operation of this magnitude for so long without a trace . . . that she could have actively overseen the millions of details undetected, despite the constant security checks that everyone at I.O. endured . . . that her long-range planning had been so many steps ahead. . . . It was staggering. But not as staggering as the big question it all raised:

If they had never suspected the existence of Gen^{14}, then what *else* might Ivana have waiting in the wings?

Ivana drank in the looks on her prisoners' faces with a self-satisfied air. "Now, if you'll excuse me," she said, smugly, "as lovely as all this catching up has been, I have a diabolical master plan to execute."

"Wait!" Kat said. "Now that you've won and you've got these kids, aren't you even going to tell us what you're going to do with them?"

Ivana looked amused. The ploy to keep her talking was

so obvious as to be laughable. How stupid did this child think she was? "No, I don't think so. Goodbye, children. It's been absolutely no pleasure at all knowing you."

Ivana spun sharply on her heel and started for the door, a jaunty spring in her step. She did so enjoy winning.

"But things didn't work out quite like you planned, did they, Ivana?"

Ivana stopped in mid-stride at the sound of Lynch's voice. She turned slowly toward him. She did her best not to show any reaction, but while the smile remained plastered across her lips, it had left her eyes. "What?" she asked.

Lynch regarded her with narrowed eyes. The others could almost see the wheels turning in his head as the pieces of the puzzle slowly came together. "Things didn't work out like you planned," he repeated.

Ivana gave him an icy look. "The last time I looked, you were chained to a wall and I was in charge. How, exactly, would you conclude that things didn't work out as I planned?"

"You were working on Gen[13] and Gen[14] simultaneously, hoping that at least one of them would pay off. But the only downside you foresaw was the possibility that one of the projects might fail to produce results. When you were tallying up the projected gains and losses, the loss column never went much beyond a few extra corpses and a delayed timetable.

"You never expected that one of the strike teams you created would rise up to oppose you so effectively. You never expected someone like me to train them and protect them from your schemes. You never expected them to bring your tidy little position at I.O. down around your ears."

"Oh?" Ivana said, a testy edge in her voice.

"You thought you'd still be running the sci-tech division at I.O. to this day. You never pictured the gravy train ending. But thanks to these kids—your own creations—you suddenly found yourself out on the street, with none of your old 'friends' daring to admit they even knew you. Your access to those fat government pocketbooks was gone in a snap, like a little girl whose allowance got cut off.

"That's what all this is about, isn't it?"

Ivana glared at Lynch without saying a word.

"I don't get it," Bobby said.

The edges of Lynch's lips crept up. Now it was his turn for a self-satisfied smile. "Ivana's broke," he explained. "You kids beat her once too often. So now, she's got all these grand plans, but none of the resources she needs to deliver on them.

"She needs that government funding back. She needs that position of power. She needs I.O. reunited under her, bigger and better than before."

"That's nuts!" Roxy said. "Who'd be crazy enough to let her do that?"

"I can tell you who wouldn't," Lynch replied. "Among the House and Senate committees that set budget allocations, there were several key players who never would have backed Ivana or gone along with rebuilding I.O. Martin Cheswick. Charlene Sturmer. Evan Lowenthal."

Lynch inclined his head toward Ivana. "What was the phrase Sturmer used in I.O.'s budget review a few years ago? 'Science-fiction storm troopers?' "

Ivana bristled, but said nothing.

Lynch took her silence as confirmation. "All of them opposed I.O. funding, even before the problems and scandals. They certainly wouldn't have changed their minds about the organization—or Ivana—now. So over the past few months, Ivana had Gen[14] eliminate them, one by one. Each at a different time, each in a radically different way. A typical accident here, a splashy murder there. If you weren't looking for a connection, it wouldn't jump out at you. But if you knew what to look for, the signs were all there in plain sight."

"Phew. That's cold," said Grunge. "So with them dusted, Ivana just breezes on into I.O., huh?"

Lynch shook his head. "Not on a bet. After all the problems around I.O., backing Ivana would be political suicide. There's not a person on the Hill that would be caught within a mile of her."

Bobby frowned. "So what's the point? It wouldn't work anyway."

Lynch continued, undeterred. "No, it wouldn't. Not under the status quo. That's why the status quo had to change."

"I don't get it," Roxy said.

"Neither did I," Lynch admitted. "I knew there had to be a link, but for the life of me, I couldn't figure out what it was. Until just now."

"Shut up," Ivana said quietly.

"Or what? You'll kill me?" Lynch said with a wicked grin. "You're going to do that anyway, Ivana. Don't you want to dazzle us with the brilliance of your plan first? You needed a crisis—one so big that when you swooped in to the rescue with Gen[14], every political toady in Washington would be falling all over each other to jump on your bandwagon."

"That sub that sank!" Kat exclaimed.

"Sinking one sub would get some attention. But not enough for the kind of crisis Ivana needed," Lynch replied. "No, the sub was just a step. The important thing was the nuclear missile she stole from it."

Bobby gaped at Ivana. "She stole a nuke?!"

"Shut up!" Ivana's fist lashed out at Lynch's jaw. It carried a speed and strength that could only have come from the carbon steel bionics that lay beneath the artificial skin covering her arms.

Bound as he was, Lynch had no way to dodge the strike. But he could turn his head to ride with the blow and reduce its impact. Instead of tearing his head off or shattering his jaw, the punch merely left a trail of blood streaming from his lip.

Moving as one, all of Gen[13] lunged toward Ivana to defend their mentor. But the power-draining shackles crackled with energy as they held them tightly in place.

Lynch spat a bit of blood from his mouth and grinned at Ivana once more. Her reaction just proved he was on the right track. He'd struck a nerve. "Ivana needed something bigger than just a lost submarine. She needed a crisis so big that no one could ignore it. Something that would leave the whole country cowering in terror. Something that would affect everyone. So she settled on what her twisted brain told her was the perfect answer. What crisis could be bigger . . .

". . . than *World War III?*"

The color drained from the kids' faces. They had no words.

Lynch had to be wrong. Ivana was cold, sure. She only cared about herself. They'd even seen her kill her own men in cold blood when she was angry.

But World War III? Would Ivana start a war just to make herself look good? With the potential it carried for world devastation? Would she risk the fate of the entire world?

Lynch just kept talking. "What's the intended target, Ivana? Russia? No, that would have been it a few years ago. Back then, an anonymous American missile in the heart of Moscow would've started the bombs flying in a heartbeat. But there's too much cooperation between the U.S. and the Russians now. They'd believe the President's denials, and the two governments would work together to bring the missile down before it could hit.

"You need someplace that's more of a flashpoint. Iraq? Libya? Iran? Yes, one of those would do. Those maniacs are primed to release biological weapons at the drop of a hat. Not to mention Pakistan's nuclear capability. Nuke one of those countries, and the others would all be targeting America before the bomb hits the ground.

"But if Gen[14] got there in time . . .

"If they took out the enemy leaders before they could give the order for reprisals . . .

"If they ended the war before it began . . .

". . . you'd be the great savior. You could write your own ticket. They'd hand you the keys to the Pentagon—if not the White House.

"Because nobody would know that you were the one who started the whole thing in the first place."

Gen[13] waited for Ivana to deny it. They wanted desperately for her to say that Lynch was wrong. That he was miles off base.

But she didn't.

Ivana stared silently at Lynch, back in control once more. She held her head high, but the bravado didn't ring true this time. The shadow that clouded her face made it all too obvious that there were emotions seething beneath her cool exterior. The only question was whether it was regret over the course things had taken or anger that someone else could have unraveled the workings of her elaborate scheme. There was no way to tell which it was.

"You should have stayed with me, Jack," Ivana said quietly. "The things we could have accomplished together . . ."

"There was just one problem," Lynch replied. "I had a conscience."

Ivana slapped his face and stalked to the door.

Before she left, Ivana turned to face the group. Once again, she was the Ivana they all knew and recognized. "Incidentally," she said, "by all means, feel free to attempt a daring, last-minute rescue.

"It's useless, of course. Even if those restraints didn't render you powerless, events have already passed far beyond the point of no return. However, I would be deeply disappointed if you didn't try.

"It will make my victory that much sweeter when you fail."

Once she was on the other side of the door, Ivana issued a few terse orders, then strode off with a brisk, purposeful gait. The windowless halls were painted in the drab, two-tone shades of gray so typical of government facilities.

The only light came from rows of fluorescent fixtures overhead, which cast multiple shadows of Ivana, all of which changed size and shape as she walked past. Apart from the ethereal, two-dimensional images of herself, Ivana was alone.

It was only then that Ivana let her icy demeanor slip a little, betraying the shadow of doubt that even she was beginning to feel. Her doubts weren't about whether her plan would succeed. She had spent far too many hours considering and planning for all of the potential pitfalls for anything to go wrong now. With Gen[13] imprisoned and powerless, there was no one who could stop Ivana from initiating the first phase of the plan. And with her major political enemies dead, there was no one who could stand in the way of the second phase, either.

No, the doubts that were slowly creeping into her mind were of a different kind. Until a few minutes ago, despite the countless hours spent developing her scheme, Ivana had never shared the plan with another living being. The secrecy was a necessity, to ensure security, but it also meant that there had never been anyone to question the means she was using to reach her ends. And Ivana had never been particularly in the habit of questioning herself.

Seeing the plan through her captives' eyes had raised those issues, though. Ivana didn't much care what Gen[13] thought; they were nothing but a bunch of stupid kids. However, she respected Lynch. For as long as they'd known each other, Lynch had always been far too much of a boy scout for Ivana's taste. It was his greatest failing, in her view. But despite that, Lynch's long experience and icy resolve had always left her impressed. For that reason, Ivana never turned a completely blind eye toward Lynch's opinion, even if (as was frequently the case) she ended up dismissing it with only a moment's consideration.

Lynch had seen Ivana do any manner of unpleasant things over the years, and he'd never been shy about letting her know when her actions didn't match up to his personal, high-handed standard of morality. Yet, she could tell from Lynch's manner that this time was different. To his way of thinking, this time, Ivana had crossed a line.

Was it true? Had she raised the stakes too far this time?

To be honest, the question had never crossed her mind before. It wasn't as though she had begun with the idea of starting a World War. At first, Ivana's thought had been merely to create a generation of secret gen-actives who could be useful in implementing any number of her planned operations. If secrecy demanded terminating the technicians who had assisted her in the process, well, that was simply the cost of doing business. And if some short-sighted politicians were going to stand in the way of her goals, then it was easy enough to eliminate them as well. A few more corpses added to Ivana's body count weren't about to cause her to lose any sleep.

Things had progressed from there. In retrospect, Ivana could see the hundreds of small steps that had escalated to the point where, when she realized that she needed a truly global threat for Gen[14] to overcome, a nuclear war seemed like the most reasonable option. Since Ivana fully expected Gen[14] to prevent the war, the potential risk appeared to be minimal. However, Ivana had never stopped to think about the massive loss of life that the missile would cause on the "other side," even if her operatives succeeded in pre-empting any retaliation. The casualties had been nothing more than a vague abstraction, half a world away.

Until now.

For the first time, Ivana felt heavy with the prospect of so much blood on her hands. Lynch had been wrong about Ivana having no conscience. She merely subscribed to a different system of values than he did. Ivana's conscience most certainly existed, and it was active now. It nagged at her, asking whether she had it in her to carry through with her plans . . . and, equally important, whether she should.

As Ivana approached the command center that ran the complex, she weighed the ultimate benefits of the operation against its losses. The fact was (Ivana told herself) that she wasn't just doing this for herself. This country—the world, for that matter—suffered from a lack of strong leadership and discipline. Ivana had studied the people in power, the select few who ran the world, with a scientist's eye. She had observed some of them up close and others from a distance, but without exception, what Ivana found among them did not particularly impress her. It was painfully clear to her that someone needed to step in and set things on track. So far, she had failed to find anyone as qualified to do that as herself.

True, achieving those goals came with a price. Lives—many lives—would be lost. But, Ivana felt, anyone who looked at the situation objectively would have to label that region of the world as a powder keg. With all of the wars, factions, and in-fighting that erupted there on a daily basis, how many of those people could be reasonably expected to fill out their natural lifespans anyway?

Looking at it that way made the answer obvious. Yes, thousands would die. But they would be giving their lives in the service of a greater cause—a cause that would benefit billions. When you set it in context, the price was well within the parameters of what a military commander would term "acceptable losses."

Ivana held her head high as she reached the security checkpoint outside the command center. She waited for the automated lasers to probe her retinal patterns and confirm her identity.

Only one issue remained in Ivana's mind: Could she bear the weight of so many deaths on her conscience? Could she live with herself, knowing that she'd ended so many lives?

As the door slid open to admit her, Ivana knew that there was only one possible answer:

She had to.

She owed it to the world.

•   •   •

"I thought she'd never leave," Bobby remarked dryly.

"So . . . now what?" Roxy asked.

It was a reasonable question. Ivana had gone, but the video camera continued to keep track of them—assuming, of course, that anybody was bothering to watch the video feed at this point. They were still hanging from the wall by metal restraints. Their bonds continued to cancel out the effects of their gen-factors, leaving them powerless. No one else knew where they were (for that matter, they didn't even know themselves), so there wasn't going to be any back-up team swooping in to the rescue. And no one outside this cell suspected just how precariously the world was teetering on the brink of nuclear annihilation— or, perhaps even worse, "salvation" at the hands of Ivana Baiul.

Things didn't look good.

Yet, it was a mark of Gen¹³'s determination that, even with the odds stacked so heavily against them, none of the heroes had resigned themselves to losing. None of them had given up. They knew they had to stop Ivana. They just didn't know how.

All eyes turned to Lynch.

The team's mentor studied his young proteges thoughtfully. "All of you, try using your powers for a minute."

"But, these chains . . . ," Grunge protested.

"Try anyway," Lynch said.

None of them really saw much point to Lynch's order. Each of them had already tried on his or her own, without success. But they knew enough not to question Lynch's orders, and besides, it looked like he had some kind of plan in mind. So they gave it a try.

Once again, Roxy strained to rise barely an inch or so into the air.

Bobby conjured up nothing more than a few sparks from his fingertips.

Kat pulled her bonds taut, but only caused them to creak a little before she had to release the pressure with a grunt.

Patches of Grunge's skin started to take on the color of the wall behind him before fading back to normal.

A slight breeze rose up around Sarah, but it was hardly enough to disturb the dust beneath her feet.

Lynch nodded. "Perfect," he said.

"Huh?" Kat said. The others looked equally confused. Compared to their usual power levels, their current performance struck them as kind of lame. It wasn't as though Lynch had a habit of expecting less from them than they did themselves. Usually, he was the one who was constantly pushing them beyond their limits. How could Lynch possibly consider such pathetic results "perfect?"

He read the question on their puzzled faces.

"Ivana knows more about you kids and your powers than almost anyone else on Earth," Lynch explained. "Odds are, she's calibrated these dampeners to each of your individual power levels."

"And that's a good thing?" Grunge asked.

"In this case, yes," said Lynch. "Remember, Ivana hasn't had the chance to monitor you closely since you broke out of her Project Genesis facility. That was a long time ago. Any more recent information would only be an estimate based on field observations."

Kat's eyes lit up. "That's right! She's got loads of data on us, but it's all from when we first went gen-active. We've gotten stronger since then."

"Right. By exercising your abilities, and through the training I've given you, your power and control have increased since then. Not tremendously, but enough to make a difference."

"That's why we can manifest our abilities slightly, even with the dampeners," said Sarah, catching on.

"Fat lotta good that does us," Grunge said. "So we're gonna be all like, 'C'mere, Ivana, so I can singe your eyebrow?'"

"I had a more effective plan in mind," said Lynch. "Unfortunately, Ivana had Gen[14] confiscate my lockpicks when I was captured. So we'll just have to make do with the materials at hand."

Bobby looked around, stumped. " 'Materials at hand?' " he wondered aloud. "What materials at hand?"

"Step one is to buy ourselves a little privacy. We have to eliminate that camera," Lynch said. He pointed at the thin wire that led from the camera into the wall. "Roxanne, you need to focus your power on that cable. Make it heavy enough to pull itself loose from the camera."

Roxy looked up at the wire. Lynch was right. It wouldn't take that much additional weight to rip it out. Ordinarily, it would take about as much effort as blinking. Under the circumstances, though, the thing that made it tricky was the distance. The camera was clear across the cell. With her powers inhibited, projecting that far wouldn't be easy.

"I'll try," she said.

"Trying isn't enough," Lynch replied. "You have to *do* it."

Roxy nodded. She closed her eyes to minimize the distractions. She imagined the wire before her. With a deep breath, Roxy focused her thoughts.

Nothing happened.

Roxy's brow furrowed. She concentrated harder, focusing on a single point in the middle of the wire.

Still nothing.

Then, without warning, the wire seemed to give the faintest twitch.

Roxy gritted her teeth and poured it on. Under normal circumstances, working this hard would make a building collapse.

Slowly—painfully slowly—the wire lost its slack. Little by little, the midpoint of the wire began to move. It descended, pulling itself downward into the shape of a V.

Roxy held her breath. Her face reddened with the effort.

Suddenly, with a small burst of sparks, the wire tore free. The red light on the camera went out.

The team erupted into cheers. "All right!" "Nice one!"

Roxy grinned, sweating and catching her breath.

Lynch's voice broke off the festivities. "We're not done yet," he said. "Even if no one is actively monitoring the feed from that camera, they're bound to notice the lost signal before long. They may rush the room right away, or they may wait a bit before going in blind. But either way, we don't have much time. Grunge!"

"Yo!"

"You're going to be my lockpick."

"Huh?"

"Absorb the molecular structure of your restraints. I need you to turn two fingers into metal rods thin enough to fit in these locks and long enough to reach Kat's manacles."

Grunge looked across Lynch at Kat. She was only about four or five feet away, but it might as well have been a mile. "You're kidding me," he said.

Lynch didn't have to say anything in reply. His glare spoke volumes. It said that he wasn't kidding. It said that Lynch had neither the time nor the patience for Grunge's nonsense. And most of all, it said, *Do it now!*

So Grunge did.

Or he tried, anyway.

Just as he had seen Roxy do before him, Grunge took a deep breath and closed his eyes. He held out his left hand, the one closest to Kat, stretching as far in her direction as the restraints would allow. He directed his attention toward that hand, and at the metal restraint that circled his wrist. He concentrated, trying hard to force the change.

At first, nothing happened.

The others stared, watching for some telltale shift in the color or texture of Grunge's skin that would signal the process beginning.

His fingertips started to shine. The room's fluorescent light glinted off his fingers as they began to take on a smooth, reflective veneer. Grunge's fingers began to narrow . . .

. . . and he lost it.

The moment was broken. Grunge panted for breath as his hand instantly reverted to its normal form.

Grunge shook his head. "Sorry," he said. "I tried. But it's just too much. I can't . . ."

"You *have* to," Lynch said. The tone of his voice left no room for question or debate.

Grunge glanced over into Lynch's cold, unflinching stare, then sheepishly looked away. He looked around toward his friends for support, but found only their pleading eyes.

Bobby spoke quietly from beside him. "Listen, Gee," Bobby said, "you've gotta do this. You're our only shot at getting out of here. Without you, we're toast."

"Dude," Grunge replied, without looking at him, "I tried. I don't wanna let you guys down. But what can I do? It's impossible."

"Nah," Bobby said, in a tone that was lighter than his actual mood, "it's not impossible. It's really, really hard, that's all. But it's not impossible. The Grunge-man can do it. You're not gonna let Ivana's toys stop you. You da man, right? You can do this. Hey, after all . . .

". . . all it takes is will power."

Will power.

Grunge's mind flashed back to the scene outside the movie theater. Had it really been only yesterday? It seemed like a lifetime ago when they were playfully bickering and making bets. *I'm all about will power*, Grunge had proclaimed. *I'm the very model of will power!*

I'm the mack daddy of will power!

Well, now it was time to prove it.

Grunge puffed up his massive chest. "All right," he said. "Stand back! I'm going in!"

Once again, Grunge closed his eyes. But it was different this time. Every bit of body language showed it.

Grunge relaxed his neck, letting his head tip forward until his chin was resting on his chest. It had been a long time since Grunge actively studied martial arts, and

Bobby had been right about his ultimately getting kicked out of the dojo for lack of discipline. But the thing that his sensei never understood was that Grunge's lack of discipline was just his nature. It didn't mean he hadn't been paying attention.

Grunge called upon that training now, as he drew upon the hidden reservoirs of energy that lay deep within. Grunge breathed deeply and focused his thoughts. He visualized the energy flowing up and through his body.

Roxy watched him with an expression that showed both hope and concern. With all her heart, she wished there was some way to make this easier for him. To lend him strength.

Under her breath, Roxy began to chant: "Go, Grunge. Go, Grunge. Go, Grunge. Go, Grunge."

Bobby looked over at Roxy. The chant took him by surprise at first, but then he grinned. He quietly joined in with her: "Go, Grunge. Go, Grunge."

Before long, the entire team had taken up the chant, encouraging Grunge and cheering him on: "Go, Grunge. Go, Grunge. Go, Grunge. Go, Grunge."

Grunge smiled, but kept his eyes closed. He couldn't afford to let himself get distracted. In his mind's eye, Grunge could see the power now and channel it as he wished. He drew it from throughout his body and focused it like a laser, feeding it all into the index and middle fingers of his left hand.

Grunge's hand began to change.

Once again, his fingers took on the reflective sheen of his manacles. But this time, it wasn't a fleeting glimpse. This time, it stayed.

As the change became apparent, the chant grew faster: "Go, Grunge. Go, Grunge. Go, Grunge. Go, Grunge."

Now for the hard part, Grunge thought.

Grunge had made the change, all right. But his fingers were still only inches long. Kat was several feet away.

Grunge's jaw tightened. He felt the pressure in his forehead build. But he had found his inner well of power now—he had found his *chi*—and he was in the zone.

Slowly, Grunge's fingers started to narrow. They started to grow.

"Go, Grunge. Go, Grunge. Go, Grunge. Go, Grunge."

By the time Grunge's fingers reached Lynch, they were half their normal width. Grunge's entire body glistened with a thin film of sweat. He concentrated still harder, trying to keep the process going without pushing so hard or fast that he'd choke and lose it.

"Go, Grunge. Go, Grunge. Go, Grunge. Go, Grunge."

Grunge's body trembled with the effort. The tremors made the winged skull tattooed on his chest look like it would take flight at any moment. But despite the strain of the herculean effort, Grunge was past the wall now. There was no way that anything was going to stop him.

"Go, Grunge! Go, Grunge! Go, Grunge! Go, Grunge!"

"Good!" Lynch said, tersely. "That's it! Hold it there!"

Grunge's fingers had become a pair of five-foot-long wires. They retained the same tensile strength as the metal in the manacles he had mimicked. However, stretching them out so far had made Grunge's fingers as thin as two pieces of string, bobbing gently under their own weight.

Grunge kept his eyes closed, laboring to keep his fingers in their current shape and form. With so much of his strength drained by the restraints, the slightest break in his concentration would snap them back to normal in an instant.

Now, it was Lynch's turn.

Lynch strained forward to grab the pair of wires in his hands. He instructed Kat to extend her own hands as far toward him as possible. She responded immediately. But even so, there was still a gap of a couple of feet between her wrists and Lynch's hands.

Trying to pick the locks on Kat's manacles at this distance was going to be like trying to pick up a grain of rice with two pool cues as chopsticks. Still, as Lynch had told his charges, there was no choice here. Lynch couldn't just try. He had to do it. And he had to do it fast.

It took several attempts—and precious time—just to guide the pair of wires into the small keyhole on the side of Kat's right-hand manacle. Once he'd gotten that far, Lynch used the wires to probe around the inside of the lock, feeling his way around the tumblers. If the mechanism was as simple as the lock on a pair of handcuffs, he could manage it relatively quickly and easily; in that case, he could probably pick the lock with just one wire. However, if it was anything more complex—even something like what might be found inside a simple padlock—he'd need them both.

Unfortunately, a few seconds was enough to tell him that it would take both.

"Keep your hand still," he told Kat.

Lynch set to work. No one who knew John Lynch would have described him as a gentle man. Nevertheless, he manipulated his tools with a delicacy and fine touch that impressed his young proteges and always took them a little by surprise when such opportunities arose.

One of the first things that any observer would have noticed was that, oddly, Lynch appeared to be staring blankly off into space instead of looking at what he was doing. However, the reality was very much to the contrary. At this distance, Lynch wasn't able to see inside the lock, so he needed to work by touch. Looking at the lock would only have provided useless sensory information that would have distracted him more than it would have helped.

Time and again, Lynch gingerly pressed down on the individual tumblers inside the lock. He raised and lowered them by fractions of millimeters as he experimented with different combinations of arrangements, until, finally, he felt something give.

Kat's manacle popped open, sending her off-balance. She swung awkwardly down and around to the left, now suspended by only three restraints, until she caught her balance. She grabbed the left-hand chain with her free hand, and used the strength of both hands to force the left-hand manacle as close to Lynch as possible.

Once again, there was a chorus of hoots and cheers. "All right!" "Way to go, Mister L!" "Woof! Woof! Woof!"

Now, Lynch had to do it again for Kat's other hand.

The process went more quickly the second time around. Lynch knew how the locks worked now, and as he had hoped, the same key appeared to work for both manacles. That meant far less experimenting, which, in turn, meant far less time.

Before long, Kat's second manacle sprang open as well. This time, though, she was ready for it. Clinging to the left-hand chain with her right hand helped her to keep from losing her balance again and landing on her face on the floor.

"Cool!" Roxy said. Her face looked as enchanted as if Lynch had just pulled a rabbit out of an empty top hat. "Now do her feet!"

"No need," Lynch replied. "The dampeners are only wired to the wrist restraints."

Kat glanced down and quickly confirmed Lynch's words. It was true. The thin cables that wove through the wrist chains weren't there for the restraints that bound her ankles.

Kat smiled to herself. Although she was free of the power dampeners, it would still take a few minutes for her to regain enough of her strength to tear apart the metal restraints. But pulling them out of the stone wall . . . well, that was another thing entirely.

Kat switched the chain to her left hand and slipped her right hand under her thigh. She bent her knee and began to pull her leg upward in a smooth motion, as hard as she could. The heavy metal resisted her. But she combined the strength in her arm with the muscle power in her leg, and simultaneously pulled down on the chain with her left hand to increase the leverage.

Under that kind of pressure, it didn't take long. There was a shrieking sound, like nails on a blackboard, and an explosive, crumbling noise as the stone around the restraint gave way. Her right leg came free.

Kat let go of the wrist chain and dropped down the short distance to the floor. She hopped around to face the restraint that still trapped her left leg. Awkwardly, she crouched down to take the chain in one hand as she pressed the palm of the other hand flat against the wall. With all the strength she could muster, Kat pulled with one hand while pushing with the other.

In seconds, she was free.

Now that she was away from the power dampeners, Kat's strength was growing closer to normal with every passing moment. It was relatively straightforward for Kat to work her way down the row, tearing open the metal restraints that held each of her fellow prisoners. Not that the tempered steel made it easy, of course. But compared to what she had been through so far, it was a walk in the park.

One by one, Kat's friends joined her on the floor, stretching the muscles in their aching shoulders and massaging their wrists to restore the circulation.

As Kat moved on to Sarah and Roxy, Bobby walked over to Grunge and gave him a friendly clap on the back. "Yo, Grunge-man."

"Hey."

"Nice will-power action back there. You really came through for us, y'know? *Tres* impressive."

"Like I said, dude. I am the mack daddy of will power."

"Yeah. I think you might just be," Bobby said. "Hey, listen. You know that bet?"

"Yeah?"

Bobby grinned and winked. "Forget it."

Grunge raised an eyebrow in surprise, then returned the grin. "Thanks, dude," he said. "Now, about that Michelle Yeoh . . ."

"All right, people, listen up," said Lynch. Kat had freed Sarah by now, and was just finishing up with Roxy. "If they don't already know we're free, they will in a minute. Priority one is stopping that missile, not avenging your bruised egos or trying to prove you can take Gen[14] in a fight. Got it?"

The team nodded their assent. Some of them nodded grudgingly, but they nodded nevertheless.

"That said," Lynch continued, "getting to Ivana is almost certainly going to mean fighting our way past Gen[14]. Watch yourselves—those kids are more powerful than you are, and probably fresher, too. They haven't spent the past several hours hanging from a wall."

"Thanks for the pep talk, Coach," Grunge muttered under his breath. However, the fact that he was still rubbing his sore muscles was enough to remind him that Lynch was right.

"But there may be a vulnerable point that we can exploit to our advantage," Lynch said. "Remember, these kids were trained by Ivana. She was the head of sci-tech at I.O., not a combat branch. Tactics and strategy aren't exactly her field of specialization."

The words struck home for Kat. During their last battle, it had already begun to dawn on her that Gen[14] was using the exact same strategy every time they fought. In each battle, the opposing team had split into pairs or trios to outnumber and attack each member of Gen[13] individually. Kat hadn't caught on immediately, because the pairings varied each time. But it was a recurring trend, with every one of the match-ups hand-picked to counteract the heroes' individual abilities.

Maybe Lynch was right. Maybe that pattern could be anticipated and exploited somehow . . .

"Okay, we're on the clock," Lynch said. "Let's get out of here."

Sarah stopped massaging her broken ribs. Hanging from her arms for so long hadn't done them any good. But there was no time to worry about that now.

Kat reared back to strike the door with a powerful side kick while Roxy negated its weight. The reinforced, three-inch-thick door flew off its tracks and across the hall outside to smash into the opposite wall. It fell flat on the floor with a resounding clang.

Gen[13] poured out the door into the hall.

Gen[14] was there waiting for them.

"Let's rock and roll," said Grunge.

CHAPTER 13

E qual numbers of the Gen^{14} kids had been stationed to either side of the door. The escaped prisoners were surrounded on all sides, with no way out.

"Go," said Highwire.

Without another word, Gen^{14} swarmed in to the attack. Thoughts were flying through Fairchild's mind, making it seem as though time had slowed to a crawl, as her head swiveled back and forth to observe and analyze their offensive. Like a well-oiled machine, the Gen^{14} kids were once again peeling off into pairs to hit the heroes, two to one. Each pair was comprised of one kid from the left-hand group and one from the right. Every one of them knew his or her individual target and was bearing down for the kill like a pinpoint laser.

In a matter of seconds, Grunge was writhing on the floor under Rave's sensory assault.

Before Rainmaker could summon up the fury of a rainstorm, Riptide's watery form was already blasting her off her feet with the force of a tidal wave.

Freefall was clutching her ears, trying in vain to protect herself from the noise. But that didn't stop her body from spasming violently under Reverb's vibratory assault.

Under Override's control, Burnout had taken to the air near the ceiling and was peppering the battlefield with bursts of white-hot plasma. Fairchild saw Lynch leap out of the way of one of his fiery blasts, scant heartbeats before she leapt for cover herself.

It's happening again! she thought with alarm. An awful sense of *déja vu* crept over her like an icy hand. She could see that this fight was going to end every bit as badly as the ones that had come before. It was the same thing all over again.

The same thing . . .

That's it! Fairchild thought.

It all came together in a flash. Knowing their opponents' strategy meant that they could anticipate it, and turn their own tactics against them. All at once, Fairchild knew what they had to do, and how to beat Gen¹⁴. It was just like Lynch had said—the key was in Ivana's training. She'd trained the Gen¹⁴ team, but Ivana had never been much of a team player herself. For that matter, neither had her Gen¹³ pets, Threshold and Bliss. The exact same blind spot screamed out in the tactics that Ivana had drilled into Gen¹⁴.

Sure, the Gen¹⁴ kids attacked in pairs. But that didn't mean they attacked *as* pairs. If they were truly functioning as a team, they'd be complementing each other's strengths and compensating for each other's weaknesses. But they weren't. Every time the two generations of gen-actives had met, Gen¹⁴ had been fighting tag-team style, as individuals, instead of as a unit.

Not that Gen¹³ had been doing things much differently. For the most part, they'd been so busy reacting and defending themselves that they'd mostly been fighting as individuals, too . . . and getting overwhelmed and outgunned as a result. But every time they did work together—escaping the apartment, the rescue at the interview—they'd always come out on top.

Because if there was one thing Gen¹³ knew about, it was teamwork.

It wasn't something they had learned back at I.O., from Ivana and her crew. It came from Lynch's endless training sessions, from countless battles with enemies far more powerful than themselves, and most of all, from the trust in each other that had grown with their friendship.

The abilities that stemmed from their individual gen-factors made each member of Gen[13] formidable. But it was teamwork that made them unbeatable.

"Don't fight them alone!" Fairchild called to her teammates. "Watch each other's backs!"

Just as Bogeyman was about to get a lock on Fairchild, she lowered her head, crouched down, and charged to the attack. Bogeyman prepared to duck out of the way of the charge.

But Bogeyman wasn't the one she was attacking.

Rave was so focused on her mind-bending assault on Grunge that she never even saw Fairchild coming. The three hundred-pound heroine hit with the strength and speed of a runaway freight train. If the impact of the collision didn't knock Rave out, slamming into the wall surely did.

"Not the most satisfying win of my life," Fairchild remarked to herself, "but it serves the purpose."

With Rave unconscious, the world suddenly flooded back to fill Grunge's senses. He shook his head, his long hair flying, as he took it all in. "Whoa, what a trip," he muttered. "Speed kills."

Just then, Grunge spotted Freefall shaking and spasming out of control. "No way," he growled. Grunge touched his fingers to the thick sole of his high-topped workboot and leaped into the fray with a hearty *"HAIIIIIIII-YAA!"*

Reverb turned at the sound of the battle cry (as did almost everyone else, actually), just as Grunge struck him in the chest with a flying kick. "Bam!" said Grunge, completing his follow-through to land on his feet. "Who's your daddy?"

Reverb hit the ground hard, but recovered quickly, rolling with the impact. Even as he regained his footing, he hammered Grunge with a devastating sonic blast . . . that had no noticeable effect whatsoever.

Grunge grinned and lifted his shoe. "Rubber soles, dude."

Reverb started as he suddenly realized that Grunge's skin was jet black instead of its usual color. Nor was it

skin anymore. Grunge had become pure rubber from head
to toe—shock-absorbent rubber that could absorb the vibrations from Reverb's blasts.

"Time to go 'unplugged,' dude," said Grunge. With
that, he delivered the knockout blow.

Grunge stood over his fallen foe for a minute, enjoying
his victory . . . but not for long. He howled in pain as a
ball of Burnout's fiery plasma hit him in the back and
side, and stuck there like napalm. The heat was intense
enough to melt the part of his body where the plasma
adhered. Grunge's rubbery skin turned into foul-smelling
goo in a cloud of acrid, black smoke.

Freefall knew she had to do something. She had to stop
Burnout.

Uh-uh, she corrected herself. *I have to stop Override.*

Freefall turned to face Override, who was standing off
to the side, immobile, while she controlled Burnout's
body. Before Override knew what was happening, Freefall
pointed at the twelve-year-old puppet mistress and sent
her soaring up into the cement ceiling, then doubled her
normal weight to send her crashing to the floor.

With Override unconscious, the fiery barrage came to
an abrupt halt as Burnout seized back control over his
body. Without a moment's hesitation, he turned his power
to the place where it would do the most good.

Rainmaker was sprawled on the floor near the wall,
dazed, sputtering, and coughing up water from Riptide's
blasts. As though Riptide's attack wasn't bad enough on
its own, every one of the racking coughs made her broken
ribs grind together, sending a fresh wave of pain through
her body. Riptide readied another attack, morphing his
arms into dual jets of cascading water to batter his helpless foe.

Assuming they reached her, that is.

Halfway there, the jets of water vaporized into steam
under the heat of a searing bolt of flaming plasma. Riptide
screamed, seconds before Burnout swooped down to finish him off with a roundhouse punch to the jaw. Riptide

crumpled to the ground, unconscious, with clouds of water vapor drifting harmlessly in the vicinity of his shoulders. Even once he woke up, it would take time for him to pull himself back together.

As the battle raged on all sides, Gen^{13} seemed most focused on defending themselves against the most immediate threats. So once he lost his chance to strike at Fairchild, no one seemed to be paying much attention to Bogeyman. That, he reasoned, was an error. For even if he had lost Gen^{13}'s team leader for a moment, he could go one better.

Bogeyman locked eyes with Lynch.

Lynch had been standing only a few feet away, but he'd been distracted by the chaos around him. Bogeyman didn't waste any time. The instant he made contact, Bogeyman reached deep into the recesses of Lynch's soul. He dredged down for the darkest, most terrifying secret fears he could find, then wrenched them up to put them on display.

In the past, Bogeyman had seen many reactions to his efforts. Some had screamed. Some had run. Others had gone mad. Martin Cheswick had thrown himself out of a seventeenth-floor window.

Lynch smiled. A nasty smile.

"Nice try, kid," Lynch said. "Sorry to disappoint you, but I faced my deepest fears years ago. They're old friends. Now, it's your turn to give it a try."

Nothing like this had ever happened to Bogeyman before. No one had failed to succumb. Nothing in his training had prepared him for something like this.

Lynch started toward him. Lynch wasn't hurrying. His expression said he didn't need to. He stepped toward Bogeyman at a deliberate pace.

The twelve-year-old's normally impassive face went pale. As Lynch loomed over him, Bogeyman turned to flee.

He found Freefall standing behind him. "Aw, c'mon, Mister L," she said. "Let me."

Before Bogeyman could react, Freefall leapt a good five feet straight up in the air. Gravity ceased to exist beneath the teen as she did a tight, 360-degree spin, then multiplied her weight as she lashed out with her foot to make contact with Bogeyman's jaw. Bogeyman went down in a motionless heap.

"Eat your heart out, Michelle Yeoh."

Roxy stared at the limp form at her feet. Fighting back—not out of fury, but out of simple determination—had left her feeling cleansed. She still remembered every bit of what he had put her through, but it didn't feel so bad anymore. "Oooh, mondo creepy bogeyman," she said, not quite keeping the shiver out of her voice. She gave what she hoped was a cool, indifferent shrug. "As if."

A short distance away, Grunge screamed as Slash's razor-sharp arm tore through his already-damaged rubber torso. The blade left a wide gash in its wake, cutting clear through half of Grunge's abdomen. Grunge clutched the loose ends to hold them together.

Slash reared back to finish the job. But before he could deliver the blow, he found himself sailing through the air in the grasp of a force-three hurricane. Rainmaker blew Slash all the way down to the end of the hall. As the blank wall rushed to meet him, Slash raised his arms to protect himself.

However, in the heat of the moment, Slash didn't realize that raising his arms was exactly what Rainmaker was planning on. Like straws driven by a hurricane, the twins blades met the concrete wall . . . and plunged straight through. By the time the wind died down, Slash was trapped, wedged up to his shoulders in the solid wall.

Freefall rushed to Grunge's side. "Pookie!" she shouted. "Are you okay?"

Grunge winced with pain. "This's really . . . gonna . . . sting . . . in the morning."

Freefall breathed a relieved sigh. If Grunge had been in his human form, either the burns or the gash would have been more than enough to kill him. In his many morphed forms, though, he'd survived worse than this. She couldn't begin to imagine the pain he must be feeling from the combined attack, but he'd be all right. Grunge just needed time—first some time to put himself back together and switch back to human, and then some more time to recover.

Unfortunately, time was something they didn't have right now.

Freefall looked up to see Knockout bearing down at them at full speed. Freefall had less than a second to prepare to defend her man.

But Burnout got there first.

"Incoming!" he yelled.

Burnout conjured up a fiery mass of plasma that wrapped itself around Knockout's head. Knockout fought a wave of panic as she halted her charge and started trying to beat out the flames. Yet, after a moment, she realized what Burnout had already figured out: Her super-strong body was far too tough to be injured by the white-hot plasma.

In fact, Knockout realized, the flames were more of a nuisance than anything else, blinding her so that she couldn't resume her attack. Still, if that was the case, she intended to make sure that no one else would take the opportunity to attack her, either. She flailed about blindly with her arms and legs, intending to drive off anyone who might be tempted to get too close.

Still flailing around, Knockout started to cough. Yet, even after that, it took her another minute or two to realize, wide-eyed, where the real threat lay.

No, the fire around her head couldn't hurt her. But it could eat up the oxygen she needed to breathe.

Instantly, Knockout dropped her defensive action and went back to trying to smother the flames with her hands. Every time one bit of the plasma went out, though, Burnout simply added more on. It was a variation on the same attack that Riptide had used on Fairchild back on the street. And it worked every bit as well on Knockout now.

The harder she fought, the faster she used up the oxygen in her lungs.

Before long, Knockout sank to the floor. Her attempts to beat out the flames grew more and more sluggish, until, finally, she passed out from lack of air. True to his name, Burnout let the fire burn itself out around her.

Burnout's intervention had saved Freefall and Grunge from her attack. But taking Knockout out of the picture didn't leave Freefall and Grunge safely out of the woods, either. Growing Boy had snatched Freefall up in his massive hands and squeezed. The pressure was incredible.

"You . . . again?" Freefall said, through gritted teeth, as the air forced itself from her lungs. "Y'know . . . you're starting . . . to tick me off . . . too!"

Freefall tripled Growing Boy's already considerable weight. Growing Boy looked down, startled, as the flooring creaked its protest before bursting under its burden. Freefall came free as Growing Boy's hands opened reflexively in surprise. He fell through the floor to the level below. His gargantuan size prevented his entire body from plunging through, but it left him trapped awkwardly at chest height, his feet standing on the floor one story down.

As Growing Boy struggled to free himself, Fairchild leaped up to deliver a powerful haymaker. With a grunt, Growing Boy slumped down, unconscious. The only thing that kept him on his feet was the fact that he was still wedged in the floor.

With her teammates falling all around her, Sidestep had come to the conclusion that she'd better get herself out of there—and fast. Briefly, she considered a handful of possible destinations, but quickly realized that it didn't really matter. The important thing wasn't where she was going. It was getting away from where she was.

The air shimmered beside her as Sidestep created her escape hatch. But no sooner had she taken her first step toward it than the portal was disrupted by a massive bolt of lightning that coursed through it from behind. Sidestep recoiled from the blast even as the portal reformed itself.

Moving faster this time, Sidestep started to make a dash for the portal. But she stopped herself when she saw that it was now shrouded in a curtain of flame.

Sidestep turned to face Rainmaker and Burnout. Both were watching her closely. Rainmaker's hand was raised in Sidestep's direction, looking ominously like a loaded gun. Burnout stood beside her, his arms crossed, with a confident smile.

"I'm thinking this would be a good time to surrender," Burnout said.

Without warning, Sidestep howled out a battle cry as she charged the pair. Rainmaker and Burnout both started in surprise; it wasn't the reaction they were expecting. Sidestep flung herself headfirst through the air, heading straight at them.

That's when Rainmaker noticed the shimmering patch of air between them.

She felt like a total idiot. They'd fallen for the trick like a ton of bricks. She wasn't attacking. It was a feint to mask an escape through another portal. Rainmaker called up another lightning bolt, but knew it would be too late . . .

. . . until Sidestep stopped dead in mid-air. Fairchild had caught her by the ankle.

The extra second was all that Rainmaker needed. Fairchild released her grip. Before Sidestep could even reach the floor, Rainmaker hit her with a mild electrical blast. Rainmaker carefully modulated the bolt so that it didn't kill Sidestep, or even do any permanent injury. But it was more than enough to shock her into unconsciousness.

That left only Highwire.

The team leader of Gen [14] looked as though she didn't know what to do next. She hadn't expected her team to be beaten. She wasn't prepared to fight all of Gen [13] by herself. And with Sidestep down for the count, even her escape route had been cut off.

As Freefall continued to nurse Grunge, the others edged toward Highwire. She launched herself into the air, flipping over the head of a startled Burnout, then ricocheted off the ceiling past Rainmaker, and bounced off the wall to zip around Fairchild.

The evasive maneuver would have worked, too, if not for the tiny snowstorm that Rainmaker had put in her path. Highwire hit the slippery patch of snow that had accumulated on the floor. Before Highwire could even register what was happening, her feet slid out from under her and she landed flat on her back. She tried to scramble to her feet, but Fairchild was already on her knees and pinning Highwire to the ground. There was no way she could match Fairchild's phenomenal strength. Highwire was trapped, and she knew it.

Burnout and Rainmaker loomed over Highwire now, too. All three of the teens looked at her for a moment, the same thought running through each of their minds. Highwire seemed so small now, much more like a young girl than like the team leader for a gang of multiple murderers.

"Where's the missile?" Fairchild asked.

Highwire stared up at them with her jaw set and a defiant gleam in her eye. She wasn't going to tell them anything. On the other hand, she'd be very happy to spit in their faces . . . and gave it her best shot. The spittle didn't reach quite far enough.

Fairchild glanced down at the spot of saliva on her tunic and sighed. She looked down at Highwire with more pity than hatred in her eyes. "Ivana didn't even give you a real name, did she?" Fairchild said. As gently as she could, Fairchild flicked a finger under Highwire's chin. It struck with a loud *THWAK!*, snapping Highwire's head back and knocking her out.

Burnout and Rainmaker stepped back slightly to give Fairchild room as she stood up. "Guess we'll have to find the missile ourselves," Fairchild said. "Any idea where to start, Mister Lynch?

"Mister Lynch?"

They looked around. Lynch was already gone.

GEN [13]

"Looks like he meant it when he said there was no time to lose," Burnout said.

"He ran out on us?" Rainmaker said, not quite believing it.

"No," Fairchild replied. "He trusted us to win."

" 'First priority is the missile,' remember?" Burnout added.

"Odds are, he's already on it," said Fairchild. "We've got to find him and help." She looked over at Grunge and Freefall. "Grunge? Are you up to this?"

Freefall was helping Grunge stretch the loose ends of his rubber body together to make them meet. "I will be . . . in a . . . minute," he grunted. "Get that bit . . . over there . . . willya, Rox?"

Once the pieces were fully in contact with each other, Grunge willed himself back to human form. Even as the change began, the molecules that made up his chest and stomach reached out to each other. They started to knit themselves back together, bit by tiny bit. The torn shreds of rubber united to form sinews, blood, and skin. By the time the change was done, Grunge's flesh and blood body had pulled itself back together into a single whole once again.

With so much damage, though, the change wasn't easy. Throughout the process, the pain and effort showed itself through the grimace on Grunge's face. Even after he'd completed the transformation, a blackened burn mark remained where his rubber body had been melted.

One of the benefits of Grunge's gen-active nature was a healing factor that allowed his body to repair itself far more quickly than normal. On the first day his powers manifested, Grunge had been shot in the chest three times by Ivana's guards. He still remembered the pain as the bullets tore through his lungs and heart. By rights, it should have killed him. But instead, the wounds sealed themselves up within minutes. He spit up the bullets while they were still warm from friction and body heat.

Yet, Grunge's metabolism didn't make him invulnerable. The healing still took time. The more extensive the injuries, the longer the process took. And it was far from painless.

"Geez, Pookie, that looks bad," Freefall said. She reached over to touch the blackened area gingerly.

"AAAH!" Grunge screamed, jumping away. "Don't touch it!"

"Maybe you should wait here," Fairchild said, concerned. "Get some rest."

"What, and miss . . . the big . . . finish?" Grunge said, wincing from the pain. "You guys know . . . you can't make it . . . without . . . the Grunge-man." He forced a grin. " 'Sides, the important . . . thing is . . . it missed . . . my tat."

It was true. The winged skull tattoo on Grunge's chest was unsinged.

"We don't have time to argue about this," Rainmaker said. "Anybody who's coming, let's go!"

CHAPTER 14

The team raced through the halls of the vast complex en masse. Some ran. Some flew. With the world at stake, everyone was moving as fast as they possibly could.

"This place is a ghost town," Grunge said, trying his best to keep pace with the others. "Is it just me, or is this creeping anyone else out, too?"

"Ivana said the facility was decommissioned," Fairchild replied, showing no signs of getting winded as she ran. "I'd guess her helpers have been 'decommissioned,' too."

"There's, like, a zillion doors here!" Freefall complained, as she sped along without touching the ground. "How are we supposed to know which one's it?"

"Just look for the signs that say, 'This Way to Armageddon,' " Burnout replied, soaring through the air beside her.

"Mister Lynch is going to want our help," Fairchild said. "I think he'll leave the right door open for us."

"He'd better," Burnout said. "Look!"

The group slowed to a stop as they reached an intersection of two corridors. The two nearly identical hallways branched off in opposite directions.

"Bogus," said Grunge. "So now what? We split up?"

Rainmaker shook her head. "No need. I'd say it's this way."

"How'd you figure that?" Freefall asked.

"Check it out." Rainmaker pointed down one of the corridors. In the distance, they could see signs that said

"RESTRICTED AREA" and yellow and black ones with the international symbol for radioactive material.

"Works for me," said Grunge.

With that, they were back on their way.

Before long, they overtook their mentor. He was standing beside a sliding glass door and using his fingers to probe the edges of a metal panel that was embedded in the wall.

"It's about time you all showed up," Lynch said.

"Yeah, well, I stopped to do my nails," Freefall replied.

"What's that?" Fairchild asked, indicating the panel.

"Retinal scan," Lynch said. "Unfortunately, I doubt that any of us has the proper retinal pattern to open the door. And without tools, I haven't had much luck with it so far."

Kat looked through the thick glass door. The door led to a small chamber only a few feet square. On the other end of the chamber was a reinforced door, similar to the one that had been on their cell. The whole set-up reminded her of an airlock. Clearly, at one time, this had been a security post. That kind of security suggested that there was something that needed to be extremely secure on the other side.

"Bulletproof glass?" Burnout asked.

"Yes," said Lynch, "but it wasn't made with us in mind."

"That's my cue," said Fairchild, rearing back.

"No, wait!" Lynch said.

But it was too late. Fairchild punched the door with all her might. The heavy glass cracked and buckled as it flew off its track.

Instantly, the complex exploded into a pandemonium of noise. Alarms blared. Red lights flashed.

"Sorry, Mister Lynch!" Fairchild shouted over the din. "Guess Ivana knows we're coming now!"

"I'm sure she's already expecting us," Lynch shouted back. "I was thinking more of that!"

The team looked up to where Lynch was pointing. Inside the small chamber, vents near the ceiling had already started pumping out jets of sickly yellow gas. There was no way to know whether the billowing clouds were designed to leave intruders unconscious or dead. Either way, the chamber was obviously designed with the intent that the glass door would seal off the gas, preventing it from reaching anyone in the corridor. With the door broken, Gen[13] had no such protection.

"I'm on it!" said Rainmaker.

Rainmaker whipped up a strong wind, powerful enough to redirect the flow of the gas and carry it far down the hallway. But redirecting it wasn't really enough. They had to stop new gas from coming, too. Burnout studied the vents.

"Hope that junk isn't flammable," he said. "Everybody better back off, just in case."

Burnout waited for his teammates to move back and flatten themselves against the reinforced walls. Once they were safely out of the way, he hit the vents with a superheated blast. To everyone's relief, the gas neither burned nor exploded as the white-hot flame fused the vents closed. Only a small trickle of the gas continued to escape in tiny spurts.

"It's clear!" he called.

Fairchild and Freefall rushed forward and repeated the trick that had gotten them out of their cell. Freefall negated the weight of the heavy door on the far side of the chamber to reduce its resistance as Fairchild smashed it with a kick. To her surprise, the door bent inward, but stayed in place.

"This really must be the place," Fairchild muttered. Yet, even this stronger barrier couldn't stand up to a second kick. It crashed down to the floor beyond with a resounding, metallic clang.

The echo of the sound hadn't even faded before Fairchild leaped over the fallen door into the adjoining room, with the rest of the team pouring in behind her . . .

. . . only to dive for cover. A hail of semi-automatic

machine gun fire raked through the space where they'd been. Only Fairchild held her ground. The bullets hurt as they hammered her body, but they couldn't do much more than that.

The Uzi's rapid-fire muzzle flash cast an eerie light as it illuminated Ivana's features from below. Her face was twisted in a grimace of hate and frustration, but she couldn't hide the simultaneous streak of perverse enjoyment that she felt as well.

"Once and for all," she cried, "why won't you just *die*?!"

Ignoring the shower of hot lead, Fairchild raised a hand to shield her face against the barrage and looked around at her surroundings. The banks of computer consoles clearly marked this room as the launch center for the complex. Yet, even if that hadn't been enough to give it away, the huge picture window overlooking a Trident II missile would have cinched the deal. The missile stood inside an enclosed silo on the other side of the window. Only the upper portion of the missile was visible through the window. The sheer size of what could be seen—roughly seven feet in diameter, with more of the ICBM extending both above and below the window—hinted at what lay beyond. It was more than enough to send a chill down Fairchild's spine. The sight filled her with a sense of both awe and dread.

The number of chairs and consoles suggested that the launch center had been designed to be operated by a team of several people. Somehow, though, Ivana had jury-rigged it all to a central control panel so that she could run it by herself. More important, her efforts had obviously been successful, since Fairchild could already see smoke from the missile's jets rising in the silo.

Fairchild didn't know whether Ivana had already set an automated countdown in motion, or whether she hadn't yet triggered the launch. Either way, there was no way of knowing how much time was left before the missile would fly. Every second counted.

As Fairchild started toward Ivana, Ivana whipped her free hand toward her. The skin of Ivana's hand shredded from the inside as lengthy strips of molecularized razor wire shot forth from her fingers. They sailed across the room like a pack of darting snakes.

It was one of the perks of Ivana's years as head of the sci-tech division at I.O. that she had the opportunity to indulge her yen to improve her body in any way she saw fit. While many people might think of "surgical improvements" in terms of tummy tucks and nose jobs, Ivana had been inclined more toward bionic enhancements and subdermal weapons systems. Ivana's body now held more hardware than a handyman's shop . . . or a small armory. It didn't make it any easier for Ivana to pass through metal detectors without incident, but it did mean that her artificial skin concealed any number of truly nasty surprises.

Fairchild drew a sharp intake of breath as the razor wire whipped around her. It tore swaths through her uniform and drew blood from the skin that lay underneath— the same skin that even bullets couldn't penetrate. The molecularized wire couldn't cut all that deeply; Fairchild's flesh was still too tough for that. Still, the fact that it could cut her at all was enough to alert all of Gen¹³ to the danger it posed.

The lethal tendrils rose toward the ceiling as Ivana reared back for a second lunge. But before she could bring them down, Freefall yelled, "I got it!" With a gesture, she increased the weight of the wire exponentially. The strands of razor wire plummeted to the floor, throwing Ivana off-balance. As long as Freefall maintained the effect, the razor wire was no longer a deadly weapon. Instead, it served as a mass of unbreakable chains that bound Ivana to the floor.

Fairchild leaped over the inert wire to reach Ivana in a single stride. Effortlessly, she bent the muzzle of Ivana's gun with one hand, rendering it useless. With her other hand, she grabbed Ivana by the front of her blouse as the others rushed in behind her.

"You don't get it, do you?" Ivana said with a sneer. "You're too late! You've already lost!"

Lynch ran to the central control panel for the launch center. "She's already initiated the launch!" he said, his face grim.

A small, digital counter on the panel ticked off the time to launch: *00:02:04. 00:02:03. 00:02:02.*

The smoke in the next chamber was starting to thicken. The missile was vibrating faster as its engines throbbed with power.

Fairchild pulled Ivana in close. "How do we stop it?!" she yelled in Ivana's face, louder than she intended.

Ivana laughed. "You don't! I've won!

"Don't you see? I'll never give you the code to disarm it. The missile will hit its target as planned. And once that happens, the only ones who'll be able to prevent the end of the world will be Gen[14]!"

Ivana grinned nastily and added, "Of course, if you grovel sufficiently, I might consider letting you all join my team, too . . ."

00:01:57.

Fairchild looked desperately toward Lynch. His fingers were flying across the keyboard on the panel, but to no avail. "It's no good!" he said, his tone hinting at the urgency that he didn't allow to cross his poker face. "Our only hope is to either find the code or get in there and stop it manually!"

In fact, Burnout and Rainmaker were already letting loose the full force of their powers as they hammered away at the window that separated them from the missile. But the portal had been built to withstand the heat and fury of the launch of an intercontinental missile. It stood up equally well to whatever flame and lightning they could muster.

00:01:51.

"Oh, by all means, try to find the code," Ivana said, with a mocking tone. "There are only upward of sixty million possible alphanumeric combinations. How difficult could it be to find the correct one in, oh, a minute and a half?"

Grunge stroked his chin thoughtfully as he gazed at Burnout and Rainmaker, and then down at the floor. He bent down and, gingerly touched one of the strands of razor wire.

00:01:45.

Instantly, Grunge's form began to change. His skin took on a silvery, metallic hue. The outer edges of his body narrowed and tapered to razor-sharp edges. Only then did Grunge realize the one downside to his scheme, as his body sliced itself right out of his clothes. His garments fell in tatters around his now-bare feet.

"Whoops," he said.

Freefall raised an eyebrow. "Uh, pookie . . . ?"

Grunge gave a resigned shrug in reply. Without a moment's hesitation, he raced toward the window and hurled himself through the air with a cry of *"COWABUNGA!"*

Grunge extended his arms in front of him, as though diving through water. He met the window with the full momentum of his leap. The window had been reinforced against the wide-angle shocks associated with the rocket thrust that came with a missile launch. It had never been intended to stand up to a more narrowly targeted attack from a giant, man-sized blade. When you also factored in the fact that the molecularized razor wire was enough to cut even Fairchild's skin, there was no way that a window was going to turn it back.

00:01:39.

There was a loud shriek as the window parted at the impact of Grunge's fingertips. The hole widened as the rest of his body passed through. Grunge plunged through the window almost as if it wasn't there, and fell below the view of the window. With the barrier breached, the sound of the missile's engines became deafening throughout the control room.

Ivana's cool sense of triumph turned to panic. "You're

insane!" she cried over the din. "Those engines aren't designed for this! They're supposed to ignite only after
they're safely away from the sub that launches them!" She
tried to pull away from Fairchild's powerful grip, but it
was no use.

"What are you saying?" Fairchild demanded.

"I modified the system to fool the missile into thinking
it was safe to ignite the engines! The heat of the rockets
is incredible!"

"And . . . ?"

" 'And . . .' the only thing protecting us was the window you just broke! We'll all be killed!"

The color drained from Fairchild's face as she stared
at the missile. Then, she turned back to her captive, pulling her close with a look of desperate fury.

"*Now,* will you give us the code?!" Fairchild yelled.

"Never!"

A disgusted growl came from deep in Fairchild's
throat. She released her right hand long enough to punch
Ivana in the jaw. Despite the bionics that ran through
Ivana's body, the blow laid her out cold on the floor.

00:01:32.

Freefall was already squeezing her petite body through
the hole that Grunge had made. However, with Grunge's
body narrowed from the change, the opening was too
small for the others to fit through.

Fairchild reached her hands through the breach. She
used both hands to pull one side of the tempered glass
toward her as she braced her feet against the other side
and pushed. Fairchild gritted her teeth as she applied all
of her prodigious strength to the task. The window resisted her at first, but leverage was on her side. With a
loud, creaking noise, the opening slowly widened, until it
was wide enough for Burnout and Rainmaker to soar
through. Fairchild started to follow them, and was halfway
through when she stopped at the sound of Lynch's voice.

"Kat!" he shouted. "Let them do it! I need you here!"

Fairchild clambered back in through the window and

dashed to her mentor's side. "What can I do?" she called over the noise.

"We need that code, or a way to bypass it! Between your computer skills and my understanding of security systems, maybe we can figure something out!"

Fairchild nodded and took over the keyboard. Neither of them said what both of them knew. The odds of coming up with a solution in time were so slim that it would take a miracle. But it wasn't going to stop them from trying.

00:01:18.

Inside the silo, the smoke was thick enough to make it difficult to see or even breathe, let alone do enough damage to stop the missile. The hatch at the top of the underground silo was already open. Under the circumstances, the clear, blue sky that showed through the open hatch seemed less hopeful than ominous.

Freefall floated above the worst of the smoke as she poured her strength into the strongest gravity field that she'd ever created. The missile's natural weight already tipped the scale at approximately 130,000 pounds. Freefall strained to multiply that, hoping beyond hope that it would be more than the missile's rockets could bear.

Already, the only one who could bear the heat at the bottom of the silo was Burnout. He'd realized that, with the casing of the missile designed to withstand the heat of reentry, his own flame would have little chance of melting through. Instead, he added his superheated plasma to the existing heat of the jets, in the hopes that the combined temperature would be enough to fuse them shut, or at least do enough damage to prevent an effective launch.

Meanwhile, more than twenty feet above Burnout, Grunge's razor-sharp feet had torn footholds in the side of the second stage of the missile. They supported him as he used his arms to rip through the graphite epoxy casing of the missile and into whatever lay inside. Grunge had no idea what was there, or how much effect he was having, but he prayed that if he wrecked enough of it, then maybe he'd break something important.

Another twenty feet up, Rainmaker hit the missile with all the elemental fury she could muster. Even as she battered the gargantuan weapon, she simultaneously pored through her memory to recall whatever she could about nuclear missiles from the no-nukes literature she'd read. Unfortunately, though, all of the pamphlets and articles had devoted much more attention to the threats nuclear weapons posed than to ways to disarm them in a pinch. What she did remember, though, was that the detonators had to go off in a very specific way to trigger a nuclear explosion. And so, she directed her attack several feet below the nose of the missile. Perhaps she could damage the missile's guidance systems, or set off one of the detonators out of sequence. Rainmaker knew full well that if she did manage to accomplish her goal, the resulting blast could cost her life.

But even if it did, it would save millions of others.

00:00:57.
Back in the control room, Fairchild had gently pried the faceplate of the control panel loose so that Lynch could examine its inner workings. She took care not to lift the faceplate too high, to avoid severing any of the wires that led to its instruments and controls.

Lynch crouched under the faceplate to study the maze of silicon chips and printed circuits that lay within the heart of the console. He probed through it with his fingers, tracing wires from the launch clock to the relevant chip, but knowing where the wires led still wasn't enough to tell him how to stop the process. Even at a glance, it was obvious that the arrangement inside the console was far too complex to decipher in the time they had left.

Lynch stood up and shook his head. "It's not going to work," he told Fairchild over the mounting roar of the engines. "We need that code!"

Fairchild gently lowered the faceplate back into place.

She glanced over at Ivana's inert form. "But how?" she asked.

"We'll just have to figure it out ourselves!"

Fairchild looked at the launch clock. It read *00:00:51.* "There's no time!"

"We have to try!" he replied. "Think like Ivana! What would she use as a code?"

Fairchild considered that for a second. "Well, lots of times, people pick passwords that have some kind of personal meaning, so they won't forget them. What's most important to Ivana?"

"Power," said Lynch without hesitation. "Control!"

Typing faster than she ever had back in her computer classes at Princeton, Fairchild entered the words as possible passwords:

Power
Control
The clock kept going.

Fairchild kept entering related words at a feverish pace, as fast as they came to mind. Lynch barked words for her to try as well. Fairchild's fingers became a blur as they searched madly for the key to the puzzle.

Dominion
Rule
Queen
Authority
Command
Ambition . . .

None of it was making any difference. Time after time, the clock still kept going.

00:00:39.

All the while, the team in the silo continued to hit the missile with all the force they could muster. Grunge continued to gouge his way through the casing that surrounded the second stage of the missile. As he tore deeper, he found himself pulling out hunks of an oily, waxy goop from the innards of the deadly projectile. One small corner of his mind wondered what the stuff might be, but there was no time to waste on idle curiosity. As Grunge burrowed deeper still, he scooped out handfuls of the substance and let it fall to the floor below.

Then, Grunge stopped, his attention caught by a burst of flame that erupted from below. For a moment, he thought it was the missile launching, but realized otherwise once he saw that the missile continued to stay in place. *Maybe it's Bobby*, he thought, *working his fire thing down there.*

Or maybe . . .

Experimentally, Grunge pulled out another hunk of the mysterious goop. He held it to his nose and sniffed it, then recoiled from its pungent smell. Then, just to be sure, Grunge released his grip and let it drop. He watched the stuff fall until it was obscured by the smoke below him. A heartbeat later, there was another puff of flame.

Grunge nodded in understanding. Now he knew what the oily goop was. Solid rocket fuel.

A sly smile crossed Grunge's face.

00:00:27.

"It's no go! Nothing's working!" Fairchild cried.

"Keep trying!" Lynch snapped back. "We've got to be on the right track! Ivana's the biggest monomaniac I've ever met! Whatever the code is, she'd never pick anything that wasn't directly related to hers . . ."

Lynch stopped in mid-sentence. He and Fairchild stared at each other as the same thought struck both of them at the same time.

No, it couldn't be. It was too simple.

And yet . . .

00:00:21.

Fairchild typed slowly and thoughtfully. It was nothing like the lightning pace she'd used up to that point.

She entered a single word:

Ivana

The clock froze.

213

00:00:17.

Fairchild held her breath as she continued to watch the display. One second. Two.

It was true. The clock was no longer counting down.

Still, shutting down a nuclear missile isn't like flipping off a light switch. The engines didn't go silent as soon as Fairchild entered the code. But their roar was starting to die down now.

Fairchild and Lynch moved quickly to the window. They leaned through the breach and looked down to gauge the results of their efforts.

"Y'know," Fairchild said with a grin, "waiting until the last second would have been more dramatic."

"I can live without drama," Lynch replied dryly.

Suddenly, Freefall soared toward them. Grunge hovered beside her, courtesy of Freefall's gravity field, his body once again returned to flesh and bone.

"Come on!" Freefall shouted urgently. "We've gotta motor—now!"

"No, it's okay," Fairchild said. "We found the code. Everything's safe again."

"Nuh-uh!" Grunge said, looking down nervously. "We torched the fuel!"

Fairchild's eyes widened in horror. She looked down and saw flames shooting out of the side of the missile. Burnout soared up past them. Rainmaker was already up above, heading for the opening at the top of the silo.

Freefall grabbed Fairchild and Lynch by the arms and cut their weight to less than nothing. She and Grunge flew upward, pulling Fairchild and Lynch through the window and up with them.

"Wait!" said Fairchild. "What about Ivana? And Gen[14]? We've got to go back for them!"

"No time!" Freefall yelled. "That sucker's gonna blow!"

Fairchild looked to Lynch for guidance. Lynch stared silently upward, his jaw set firmly in place.

The raging fire in the silo spawned hot updrafts that

added to the effect of Freefall's negative gravity field. The two combined to push the group upward like a bubble rising through water. They sailed upward at breathtaking speed, but there was still no guarantee that it would be fast enough.

Pushing herself to the limit, Freefall widened her field upward until it encompassed Burnout and Rainmaker as well. Their weight reduced, the pair flew ever more quickly upward toward the only safe means of escape.

Back down in the launch center, Ivana began to stir. The discomfort caused by the mounting heat had been enough to revive her. Ivana swayed groggily as she raised her head to see the inferno breaking loose before her eyes. The impending disaster shocked her instantly back into full consciousness.

Her scream was a blend of rage and fear.

Ivana's scream never so much as reached the ears of Gen[13]. The team burst forth to the surface and veered off at a sharp, ninety-degree angle, putting as much distance as possible between themselves and the mouth of the silo. They landed in the snow that blanketed a surrounding field and hit the ground, flattening themselves as best as they could to protect themselves from the force of the blast that was coming.

It didn't take long to arrive. No sooner were the heroes sprawled out on their stomachs than the ground erupted with an explosion that roared like thunder. A pillar of fire shot skyward from the mouth of the silo, bright enough to make the team turn away with their eyes clamped shut. The very earth pitched and rolled beneath them.

Yet, for all the fury of the explosion, the event was equally notable for what wasn't there. Despite the fire and smoke that gushed forth like a hellish geyser, there was no telltale mushroom cloud to accompany them. Rainmaker had been right. Causing the missile to detonate incorrectly was enough to prevent a nuclear blast.

It took almost a full minute for the flames to subside and retreat back below ground. The tremors went on even longer, as the silo and underground complex collapsed in on themselves. Before long, the entire facility was entombed beneath a cascade of rocks and dirt.

Once the ground stopped quaking, it took a couple more minutes before the heroes felt secure enough to stand up. They stared in silent awe at the smoking ruins before them.

Then, as one, Gen[13] burst into a chorus of wild cheers. They hooped and hollered in abandon, jumping up and down, hugging each other, and slapping each other on the back. It wasn't just their victory that they were celebrating. It wasn't just the fact that they had saved the world from a near-doom that most of its population would never suspect existed.

No, the thing they were celebrating most was the simple fact that they were alive.

"Woo-hoo!"

"Who da man?"

"We da man!"

"Yeah!"

Grunge threw an arm around Roxy, and raised his other hand for attention. "Mad props to my sweetie," he said, "who saved our butts when it all hit the fan!"

There was another round of cheers, and suddenly, Roxanne found herself at the center of a torrent of hugs and kisses. When she could finally squeeze in a word between the accolades, she squealed, "You like me! You really, really like me!"

Despite her flippant tone, Roxy couldn't wipe the grin off her face. After the day's events, not to mention the massive outpouring of affection, all of Roxy's unspoken doubts and fears were starting to feel kind of silly. There was no denying it, even to herself: Maybe—*maybe*—Sarah and Bobby could have gotten out of the silo in time without her help. But there was no way that everyone would have made it out alive. If it hadn't been for Roxy, at least some of Gen[13] would be buried underground beneath tons of earth right now.

No matter what she had believed before, Roxy wasn't a weak link. The team needed her. More important, it was clear that they all *knew* they needed her. And more important still . . .

. . . they loved her.

"Um, speaking of saving butts . . ." Bobby pointed down at the lower portions of Grunge's naked anatomy.

"Huh? Oh. Right," said Grunge, suddenly realizing that he was shivering in the cold winter air. In all the excitement, he'd pretty much forgotten about his lack of clothes. Now that things had settled down, and he no longer had metallic skin to hide behind when he blushed, Grunge reached down awkwardly in an inadequate attempt to cover himself with his hands. Kat looked away, her cheeks a vivid crimson, but Bobby and Sarah just looked amused.

"Here, Grungie," Roxy said. She pulled off her leather jacket and offered it to him.

"Thanks," Grunge said. He took the jacket and wrapped it around his waist as best as he could. Once he had the jacket positioned the way he wanted, he used the sleeves to tie it in place. He touched the trunk of a nearby tree and absorbed its molecular structure to toughen his skin against the cold.

"Uh . . . so where do you suppose we are, anyway?" Kat said, hastily changing the topic in what she hoped would come across as a seamless segue. In fact, despite the transparent ploy, it was a reasonable question. The green fields and hills around them made it abundantly clear that they weren't in New York City anymore.

"I dunno," Grunge said with a shrug that made his brown, leaf-like hair crinkle. "Hicksville, U.S.A.?"

Roxy scanned their surroundings. "No signs of life," she said. "Not even a mall."

"Well," said Kat, "I guess we should find the nearest town, and then try to figure out a way home."

"Home?" said Bobby. "But . . ."

The team looked at each other in sudden realization. They squirmed as they cast a guilty eye toward Lynch.

"Oh, yeah . . . home . . . ," Roxy said.

"Yeah, about that . . . ," Bobby said.

Grunge put on his most innocent expression and whistled tunelessly.

Sarah took a tentative step toward Lynch. "Mister Lynch . . . ," she said, "there's something we should tell you about the apartment . . ."

Lynch had been facing away from the group, staring at the remains of the silo. He turned toward Sarah and the others with a serious look.

"Later," he said. "You can worry about figuring out where we are later, too.

"We're not done here yet."

CHAPTER 15

"**A**hhhhhhhh, this is more like it . . ."

"Nobody wake me. I'm gonna sleep for a week."

"Look—a fridge! Whadda we got in the fridge?"

By the time Gen¹³ was on their way back to New York City, they were totally wiped. It wasn't just the strain of defeating Ivana and destroying the missile. It wasn't just the battles with Gen¹⁴. It wasn't the crash that inevitably followed the adrenaline rush that came while saving the world. It wasn't even the incredible physical and emotional punishment they'd endured over the past couple of days.

It was also the fact that, after burying the underground complex beneath countless tons of debris, Lynch had insisted that they dig all the way down through the rubble to make sure that Ivana and Gen¹⁴ were really dead.

While everyone's first reaction was to look at their mentor like he was crazy, no one could really deny the fact that he had a valid point, either. They knew from long experience that Ivana had a knack for escaping certain death without so much as a hair out of place. Given that, and the fact that one of Gen¹⁴ was a teleporter, it would be both foolish and irresponsible to take anything for granted.

Still, that didn't mean they were happy about it.

Nevertheless, they did their best to blast their way back down into the underground complex. It wouldn't have been an easy task under the best of circumstances, and it wasn't made any easier by the knowledge that the damaged warhead could be spilling radiation throughout the filled-in silo. The only reasonably safe way to avoid the danger was to bypass the silo completely and dig a new way into the base, through far too many feet of dirt and solid rock.

The team gave it their best shot. But with their energies at low ebb, they never made it all that far down. Beyond a certain point, even Lynch had to admit that it made more sense to leave any further excavations to crews who were armed with the proper mechanical equipment. Even if none of them could escape the nagging feeling that no bodies would be found.

Despite forcing them into the recovery effort, however, Lynch did take good care of his charges. There was no doubt that Lynch was a tough taskmaster, pushing the members of Gen[13] beyond their limits, but he also made sure they got back to Manhattan in comfort and style. Once they'd hiked to a nearby town and established that they were in rural New Hampshire—much closer to home than it could have been, all things considered—Lynch had excused himself to use the first pay phone he found. Thanks to a telephone charge account that Lynch had set up for just these sorts of contingencies, it took only a couple of calls before he announced to the team that appropriate transportation was on its way.

Sure enough, forty minutes later, a mobile home the length of a tractor-trailer pulled up to the gas station where Gen[13] waited, attracting stares from the curious locals. How much of the attention was due to the girls' skintight costumes, and how much could be attributed to Grunge's lack of pants was a matter of opinion. Unfortunately, while Lynch could make telephone calls without ready cash or a physical credit card in hand, the same couldn't be said for buying clothes at one of the shops that lined the main drag of the small town. On the other hand, though, at least a quiet conversation between Lynch and a suspicious police officer prevented anyone from doing time for indecent exposure.

When, at last, the heroes wearily dragged themselves into the back of the vehicle, they found that its insides easily lived up to its exterior. The ride back to Manhattan was certain to take at least six hours or so. Knowing that, Lynch had arranged for all the amenities. The mobile home boasted a couple of narrow but (as Grunge immediately discovered) comfortable beds, a television, and a fully-stocked refrigerator, complete with a selection of plastic-wrapped sandwiches that matched the team's individual tastes. "Bean curd and sprouts on whole-grain bread," Bobby said. He tossed it to Sarah and continued to paw through, searching for the ham and cheese.

"Where's the beer?" asked Roxy.

"Ask again when you're twenty-one," Lynch replied.

There was even a pair of jeans waiting for Grunge. No underwear, though. Even Lynch knew that it would have been wasted on him. Grunge was much too vocal a proponent of "going commando."

Cigarettes for Roxy were similarly absent. Lynch wasn't one to lecture her on the evils of nicotine addiction, or the health hazards it posed, but he wasn't about to encourage her smoking either.

All in all, the set-up was more than enough to make the team grateful all over again for their mentor. For all the unasked questions about the mysterious connections that it must have taken for Lynch to pull this off—not to mention pulling it off in so little time—they were so happy to have it that they didn't much care.

After they were comfortably settled in for the ride, Sarah screwed up her courage and once again broached the subject of the damage to the apartment. But even then, Lynch was cool. Instead of getting angry, Lynch assured the team that it was already being taken care of. He dismissed any further discussion with a cryptic comment about his "cleaning deposit." It left them curious, but no one was too eager to press the issue in any greater detail. There was no way to know just how far Lynch's air of benevolent generosity might stretch.

In spite of the laid-back air of calm that surrounded the group, there was little of the celebratory feeling that had pervaded the atmosphere just after their escape. The adrenaline rush had worn off, leaving the group battered, dirty, and exhausted. For the remainder of the trip, they would be perfectly happy to do nothing more strenuous than eat, relax, and reflect quietly on the events of the past couple of days.

"So," Kat said, wistfully, as she wiped a spot of mayonnaise from her lip, "do you think they made it out?"

"Who cares?" Roxy replied.

Sarah was gently probing her side, double-checking again to make sure that the tape protecting her ribs had stayed mostly in place. She winced as she got to a tender spot. "Well, not about Ivana, maybe," she said. "But those kids . . ."

"Those 'kids' are stone killers," Bobby reminded them. "In some ways, it might be better if they didn't get out."

"Maybe," Kat admitted. "But raised by Ivana? What chance did they have to turn out to be anything else? I wish we could've helped them, instead of just beating the heck out of each other."

"I don't disagree," said Sarah, "but I think we have to be careful not to lose sight of something else. If Ivana and Gen[14] did survive, we're not out of the woods yet."

Each of them considered that point—and not for the first time. It was a sobering thought. No one said anything for a bit, until Lynch broke the silence.

"True," said Lynch. He'd been sitting some distance away, with his eyes closed. Obviously, though, he'd been listening to the conversation while he rested. He opened his eyes and continued. "However, if they do strike again, it won't be today. We destroyed the linchpin in Ivana's plan, as well as her current base of operations. Also, remember Ivana's motivation for setting all of this in motion in the first place. Even if Ivana survived, she doesn't have the resources at hand to rebuild overnight.

"You people did a good job today. You deserve to wait

until tomorrow before worrying about what comes next."

At that moment, everyone wheeled about at the sound of a window-rattling racket from the other end of the vehicle. Could it be another attack so soon?

Once they identified the source of the din, however, they relaxed. Grunge was sound asleep in one of the beds, and snoring loudly enough to drown out the traffic completely.

Roxy sighed. "Ladies and gentlemen, my boyfriend," she said, a contented smile on her face.

Kat stretched an arm around Roxy's shoulders, and gave her a sisterly hug. "Yes," she said. "He is."

Bobby studied his sleeping friend. A devilish grin crept over his face.

"Anyone got a marking pen?" Bobby asked. "And a dish of water?"

The long, restful trip back into Manhattan left all of Gen¹³ feeling somewhat better by the time they stepped into one of the elevators at the lavish Omni-Seasons Hotel. At least, they felt better physically, anyway. Despite Lynch's assurances, they were still apprehensive about the disaster area that awaited them up above, in their penthouse apartment. They half-expected to find the staff of the luxury hotel in the midst of moving all their worldly possessions out onto the street.

However, when they exited the elevator several dozen stories later, they were relieved to find that Lynch was as good as his word. A construction crew was already hard at work rebuilding the wall that Gen¹⁴ had destroyed. In fact, a good portion of the skeletal frame for the wall had been erected already. It would probably take a few more days to finish the work and paint it all, but they could see already that the place would soon be as good as new.

Beyond the construction workers, a clean-up crew was also on the job. Like the people working on the wall, the housekeeping people within were abuzz with activity, clearing away the debris from the battle and repairing the damage caused by the broken steam pipe.

Bobby felt a little guilty that Gen[13] hadn't been around to pitch in and deal with the havoc they'd helped cause. Bobby hadn't been raised in a privileged enough environment to feel comfortable about other people cleaning up his messes. Yet, he reasoned, these people were professionals who knew their jobs. No matter how well-meaning he and his friends might be, they would probably just be in the way. The best course of action was probably to just give the crews some space, take stock of the damage to their personal belongings, and try to get back to their lives.

That's what his friends all seemed to be doing.

Kat was already talking on the telephone. She had made a beeline straight for the phone book the instant they arrived.

Roxy was sifting through some of the rubble, and shaking the dust out of a torn afghan. "Time to shop," she said, to no one in particular.

Grunge was on his way to the bathroom.

Lynch was talking to Sarah about going for some X-rays later, just to be on the safe side. Her broken ribs would heal soon enough on their own, but Lynch wanted to be certain that there weren't any other internal injuries as well.

There was a roar from the bathroom. *Guess Grunge finally looked in a mirror,* Bobby thought, fighting to hide a smirk. *Yup, we're back to normal.*

Grunge came charging out into the living room. A pair of crude glasses had been drawn on his face in black marker, along with a jagged scar down his cheek and the word "LOSER" scrawled across his forehead in capital letters.

Grunge pointed at Bobby and glared. *"You!"* he growled.

Bobby looked Grunge over with an evaluative eye. "Nice tats, dude," he said, nonchalant. "Are they new?"

Grunge chased Bobby out of the apartment and down the hall, their mutual hoots and laughter filling the air. Roxy shook her head, bemused. She decided (not for the first time) that she'd never understand guys.

Kat hung up the phone. "Well," she said, with a resigned shrug, "so much for that job."

"Is that the one from the interview?" Roxy asked.

"Uh-huh. Even if they manage to absorb the financial hit from fixing everything from the fight, I guess they frown on prospective employees blowing up their building. Rats." She stamped down on a stray hunk of plaster, crushing it to powder. "It was such a great job, too . . ."

Roxy reached up to lay a hand on Kat's shoulder. "I'm sorry," she said. And, much to her own surprise, Roxy realized that she genuinely meant it.

Kat shrugged again. "It's okay," she said.

"So, you gonna keep looking?"

"I don't know. Maybe Mister Lynch was right, after all."

"Hmph. Imagine that," Lynch muttered under his breath.

Roxy gave no sign of hearing him. "How's that?" she asked Kat.

"Y'know." Kat gestured toward the remnants of the carnage that had torn through the apartment. "You guys needed me when Gen [14] showed up. Because of that job thing, I wasn't here."

Roxy looked at her sister for a long moment, digesting her words.

"Whoa, whoa, whoa! Reality check!" Roxy said. "You think this wouldn't have happened if you were around?"

"Well, no, that's not . . ."

" 'Cause you need to get something straight here. The way I remember it, you got your butt kicked downtown, right along with the rest of us."

"Yes, I kn . . ."

"No way can you be, like, our amazon fairy godmother twenty-four/seven."

"Rox . . ."

"And by the way, in case you forgot: We don't *need* you to!"

Kat raised her hands in surrender. "Roxy! Time out! Time out, okay?"

She paused to glance warily down at her diminutive half-sister. Roxy was doing her best to stare at Kat with a belligerent expression, but she couldn't quite keep the amusement out of her eyes.

Kat lowered her hands. "I know you guys don't need me to babysit you. You're the ones who saved *me* back at the silo and Girlsworld, remember? Not to mention a million other times before. But the thing is, if there's one thing that the past couple of days prove, it's that we all need each other."

"Big newsflash," said Roxy.

"I didn't mean for it to sound like a new revelation. It's not. But it is a good reminder. See, this job. . . . Well, it was great, but it would've taken up a big chunk of my time. A really big chunk."

Lynch was fully attentive now. Kat's words were starting to sound reminiscent of his own.

"That's just too much of a commitment. My first priority has to be here," Kat told Roxy. "Let's say I took the job. Let's say I'm working full-time, not to mention nights or weekends. Then, what if the next time around, some psycho comes gunning for us when we really need to be up to full strength—and I'm not around then, either? Not because I'm the fairy godmother, but just because we're a team?"

Kat shook her head. "It's too much to risk. You guys are more important to me than a job."

Roxy nodded slowly. "But what about all that other stuff you were saying before?" she asked. "That whole bit about needing to have more in your life than just punching out bad guys, and getting a life, and making a contribution to society and all?"

Kat looked down at her feet. ". . . None of that's changed," she acknowledged.

"So?"

Kat shrugged without looking Roxy in the eye. "I'm a big girl. I'll deal with it."

"That's not much of an answer."

"Do you have a better one?"

Sarah looked thoughtful. "Hmm. Maybe *I* do . . ."

"Caitlin, dolling, where do I push the button to look at my e-mail again?"

"Just a minute, Mrs. Blumberg. I'll be right there." Kat checked with the Mitchells to make sure they'd be all right without her. She'd been showing the elderly couple how to play an online game of bridge with another couple in Buenos Aries. After confirming that they were set, Kat got up, walked over, and with a smile, kneeled down beside the elderly woman. Placing her hand gently on top of Mrs. Blumberg's, Kat helped her guide the mouse to position the cursor in the right part of the screen. "It's right over here, see? The one marked 'Receive.' "

The cursor transformed into an hourglass as the system checked for new messages. "Oh, thank you, dolling," Mrs. Blumberg said. "I'm hopeless with these fancy machines without you. One of those old dogs with their tricks."

"Now, now, you're doing fine. It's only been a couple of weeks. Besides, you're not so old."

"That's very sweet, dolling. But you were supposed to say, 'You're not a dog.' "

Kat laughed.

The header for a new message appeared in bold on the screen. Kat pointed at the paper clip icon that accompanied it. "Look, you got an attachment."

Again, Kat gently guided her hand and helped her open the file. The old woman's face lit up. "Ach!" said Mrs. Blumberg. "Tell me, in your life, have you ever seen such beautiful grandchildren like these?"

Kat beamed back at her. "Never," she said.

Kat had lost track of the number of times she'd silently thanked Sarah for her help. Her teammate had been the one who gave Kat the idea and then made the initial connection for her. The same volunteer organization that ran the soup kitchen where Sarah devoted some of her time each week also ran all sorts of other volunteer projects around New York City, too. A Silicon Alley start-up company had donated a set of ten computers and high-speed connections to this particular senior center ages ago. But without volunteers like Kat to teach people how to use them, the machines would gather dust like so many high-tech paperweights.

In the few weeks since Kat had started pitching in at the center, it had proven to be the perfect compromise for her. Because she was working as a volunteer, Kat could spend just a few hours there each week, and if something urgent came up—like an alien invasion or a madman determined to conquer the world—her schedule was flexible. There was no money involved, of course, but that wasn't a big deal for Kat. A pay check had never been Kat's chief motivation; she was looking to make a contribution.

And if there was one thing Kat was doing here at the senior center, it was making a contribution. The feeling that Kat got from helping someone like Mrs. Blumberg connect with her grandchildren two thousand miles away was better than beating up a dozen giant, killer robots.

No question about it.

"Caitlin, dear, could you give me some help here?"

"Sure thing, Mister Jefferson."

Kat and Mrs. Blumberg exchanged a knowing smirk. Both of them knew full well that Mister Jefferson only used the computers when Kat was around. They also knew full well that he only asked her for help as a prelude to the inevitable attempt to hit on her.

It was funny. Getting hit on was the thing that Kat had tried most to avoid when she was looking for a job. But somehow, she didn't mind it so much when it came from an octogenarian in a wheelchair. The flirting felt different, knowing that he didn't really mean it seriously—at least, not completely seriously, anyway. As Mister Jefferson told Kat whenever she gently chided him on his advances, "Hey, I'm old. I'm not dead."

Kat gave Mrs. Blumberg a reassuring pat on the shoulder. The wrinkles at the corners of the elderly woman's eyes crinkled a little further as she returned Kat's smile. Then, she turned her gaze back to the on-screen image of children mugging for the camera. Kat headed off to see what sort of pick-up line Mister Jefferson would try this time.

"Hi, Mister J! What's up?"

"Ah, Caitlin, you've arrived just in the nick of time to save me from this wretched machine. And may I say how lovely you look today?"

"You say that every day."

"Can I help it if you always look lovely?"

Kat was still shaking her head when her cell phone rang. Kat had started carrying the phone when she started working at the center, and she didn't use it often. It was intended for emergencies, and in fact, only five other people knew the number. So, as soon as she heard the electronic tone, Kat excused herself to answer it.

"Hello? . . . Uh-huh . . . Again? Which building is it climbing this time? . . . Yes, okay. Where? . . . Okay, I'll meet you there. I'm on my way . . . Yes, now. 'Bye."

Kat flipped the phone closed and replaced it in her pocket as she walked over to Mister Jefferson. She gave his hand a friendly squeeze. "Sorry, Mister Jefferson, I've got to go. Something's come up unexpectedly."

The elderly man in the wheelchair looked up at her. He frowned in exaggerated disappointment. "Now? But I haven't even told you about my new yacht . . ."

"Next time, okay? But I'll warn you in advance, I don't go in much for nude sunbathing."

"Awww. You take all the fun out of life."

Kat flashed Mister Jefferson a bright smile and turned

to go. As she headed for the door, he called after her from behind: "Caitlin!"

She turned her head to look at him over her shoulder. "Yes?"

"You're a good girl."

Kat grinned at that. She was still grinning well after she reached the street.

It was true, Kat decided. She was a good girl.

But more than that.

She was a hero.

ABOUT THE AUTHOR

The product of a covert, government-sponsored experiment in genetic engineering, Sholly Fisch became a freelance writer in 1984, when his DNA was crossed with that of a typewriter. He is the author of three children's books and co-editor of an academic book on the educational impact of *Sesame Street*. His short stories and novellas have appeared in several previous anthologies published by Byron Preiss and Berkley Books: *Five Decades of the X-Men*, *Five Decades of the Avengers*, *X-Men Legends*, and *The Ultimate Hulk*. His other writing credits include numerous comic book stories (for titles ranging from *Batman Chronicles* to *Clive Barker's Hellraiser* to *Looney Tunes*), as well as television scripts, magazine articles, and material for the World Wide Web.

A developmental psychologist and former vice president at Sesame Workshop (a.k.a. Children's Television Workshop), Fisch is founder and president of MediaKidz Research & Consulting, through which he provides educational consulting, hands-on testing, and writing services for children's media. He lives with his lovely wife, Susan, and brilliantly talented children, Nachum, Chana, and Miriam.

He doesn't get nearly enough sleep.